RMS 393

Write to Me

a novel by
Patricia Ferguson

ANDRE DEUTSCH

First published 1991 by
André Deutsch Limited
105–106 Great Russell Street London WC1B 3LJ

Copyright © 1991 by Patricia Ferguson
All rights reserved

British Library Cataloguing in Publication Data
Ferguson, Patricia
Write to me.
I. Title
823.914 [F]
ISBN 0 233 98682 0

Printed in Great Britain by
WBC Bridgend

By the same author

Family Myths and Legends
Indefinite Nights

Write to Me

For Richard

One

Binnie Solway's birthday was in December, and every year her mother used to say, Tell you what, I won't get you anything now, I'll combine the two and get you an extra big Christmas present instead. But at Christmas she'd say, I can't do you anything more, it wouldn't be fair on the others; or ask her if she thought her mother was made of money.

Binnie used to dread Christmas day, because her mother always made the same promise on her birthday, and Binnie went on hoping she'd keep it, right up until the last moment; she used to lie awake hoping.

She told Will all this, when they were courting. They were on top of a bus in Holloway, on a dark November evening. She was looking down at the shops all lit up, a fruit shop glowing like a jewel box, a butcher's full of red and white shapes, as clean and neat as a miniature. The pavement was crowded, the air a twilit blue.

Binnie saw all this and it gave her such a feeling, she thinks it was just pleasure now but at the time she thought it was something else more important. She turned round and started telling Will about her birthday and all these years later she can see his face with complete clarity, because even at the time she knew he was vowing to himself that he would never offer to combine birthday and Christmas even if he wanted to get her something really expensive, that warranted it. She could almost hear him thinking it.

My birthday's in December, Binnie would think, much later, summing up this scene, putting a title across it as if it was a picture in a gallery or a book illustration. There she was, pictured with her darling in one of her life's happiest moments, the pair of them in paradise; a rosily glowing picture she has looked at more and more rarely over the years, and anyway no longer quite believes in.

Though lately, what with the new job, *My birthday's in December* and a few other similarly over-tinted scenes have been presenting themselves rather more often than usual. One or two of them occurred to her, for instance, quite recently, when she went to one morning to do Mrs Purvis.

Mrs Purvis looked as usual over Binnie's left shoulder and said, 'Tell Em to put her coat on, will you?'

Is that what she's doing? thought Binnie as she held Mrs Purvis's beaker of tea in the right place. Is it a memory she's somehow got stuck with?

Tell Em to put her coat on, will you? It was all Mrs Purvis ever said. Sometimes she looked into Binnie's eyes as she said it, but never urgently, so it never sounded as if it might be intended to mean something else.

Whereas Mrs Bell two doors down used her one-liner, her memory's title, as a coded language. Mrs Bell said *Evidently Peter*. She wasn't senile, like Mrs Purvis. She'd had a stroke, and could think well enough, it seemed, but she could say only the one thing, 'Evidently Peter'. She said it rather often; sometimes only a bright determined running commentary ('*What* nice flowers, *isn't* it a lovely day, shall we lie you down now yes Mrs Bell?') could forestall her.

She said it in lots of different ways though. Anyone could understand her, after a while. She could say good morning, and agree or disagree, or comment on the weather just by varying tone and pitch.

It used to remind Binnie of an English textbook at school, an exercise showing how important emphasis was:

a) HAVE you taken the money?
b) Have YOU taken the money?
c) Have you TAKEN the money?

and so on. You could play with this exercise all day, Binnie thought, working out when you'd need a), or what else the person in c) thought the other chap had done with the money, merely hidden it perhaps, or torn it into bits.

Once Mrs Bell had a couple of visitors, an old man and a young one. Binnie had just gone in to get the tea tray when the old one said, 'Oh yes, we must find out how to get to the station.' Mrs Bell immediately began to tell him, waving her hands about, pointing this way and that, as she might have had she been saying, 'First right, *over* the bridge' (arch the wrist), second on your left, you can't miss it'; but all the time instead of directions she was saying 'Evidently Peter, evidently Peter, evidently Peter,' as if she was speaking another language. And yet, Binnie thought, it had all sounded quite like First right, over the bridge, second on your left, you can't miss it.

Binnie told her husband about it when she got home, and he said, 'You should put her in with the other one, see how they get on.' He meant Mrs Purvis and Mrs Bell. Binnie thought of the two of them sitting together in the lounge, both saying the same different things over and over again, Mrs Purvis vacantly, Mrs Bell getting all worked up as she always did if you didn't answer her or attended to whatever it was she wanted.

Binnie's husband held his *Daily Mail* in front of his face and sniggered, but Binnie did not bother to answer him. She thought: Perhaps that's what they were saying when something important happened, and over her lowered knitting she saw Mrs Purvis standing in some grandiose hallway, talking to the nanny, briskly or vaguely giving instructions, when – for example – her daughter fell crash! downstairs, or the cook rushed up screaming with her skirts on fire. Something sudden and dramatic, anyway, thought Binnie, to fix such a mild unconnected phrase in place.

Whereas Mrs Bell's was all due to her husband looking up from the mantelpiece (Binnie made him stand in front of the empty hearth, listlessly flicking at the invitation cards) and hoarsely saying, 'Darling, there's something I must tell you. I know all about you and that – that swine! I've been having you followed!'

And Mrs Bell, svelte on the sofa, turned another page of *Vogue* all cool and distant, and finally drawled (her heart pounding), 'Evidently, Peter!'

Well, I'm not so sorry for Mrs Bell, thought Binnie apologetically. She's still herself in some ways, has her visitors now and then. But Mrs Purvis, she's been dead for years.

Tell Em to put her coat on, will you? When it's me I'll be saying, My birthday's in December. No one will really know why, not even me. It's like, you've held on tight to the luggage label, but you've lost the suitcase, thought Binnie, going back to her knitting.

Two

When everything was ready William lifted up the headset, closed his eyes and worked the thing gingerly over his ears and into position. At once the several layers of noise all around him, occasional footsteps in the corridor outside, Gerry's subdued radio, the departmental secretary bashing away at her typewriter two doors down, retreated into a single soft roar, misty in tone like the sound that comes from a seashell.

Holding his breath against this faint damp hum William moved his hands blindly onto the keyboard in front of him and began on the start-pattern. He opened his eyes, his lashes brushing the heavy lenses. Almost immediately the image presented itself, punctual as a genie from an unstoppered bottle and just as disconcertingly ready to obey. Outlined in livid green it revolved slowly on its axis, seeming to await instruction. My wish is your command, thought William hopefully, and froze it on Frontal Aspect.

The hedge was still a bit of a joke, he decided after a pause. Vague and bulgy like something out of the *Beano*. And the suggestion of nothingness to the right was hard to ignore. But I can always put the rest of the street in later, he told himself, and his fingers on the keyboard began to tremble lightly with excitement.

Right then. Up that garden path.

Open sesame, whispered William aloud. The door fell back, disclosing the still over-long corridor, the small table halfway down it, and the closed door to the right.

On Stable Speed William passed visually into the image, reached the closed door and, still sitting on his revolving stool, turned himself slowly and deliberately to his right. Almost at once what he saw altered, nearly keeping pace, sliding obediently to the left, so that within seconds he seemed to face the closed internal door.

Sitting sideways on made it more difficult to reach the keyboard but without too much trouble William caused the door to open, and Stable Speeded himself inside. He was proud of the front room. It had taken him weeks to achieve this degree of complication. Even so it was an outing to cartoon land, set about with large single items of furniture in the snubly oblong fifties style William had found easiest to construct a programme for: a sofa, two Cubist armchairs, an entirely simple table.

Centrally within this mock-up William turned slowly to his left and back again; his compliant furniture slowly swung round too, as it should. At this success William grew skittish, and instead of backing out again crossed to the window and smoothly rose into what seemed to be empty space; the window at any rate slowly sank until he could inspect his own highly simplified attempt at a top window ledge; and moving left and backwards be began as if to swim ponderously around the room at just below ceiling level, admiring the naked lightbulb he had programmed in the day before, and all the while talking to himself rather loudly and cheerily, like a football commentator with the winning side.

'And coming up . . . yes, flying, we're definitely flying now, look mum no hands, we're heading down at those floorboards now, we're . . . off!'

So that in the professor's own laboratory next door Julia Harmon, the professor's newest postgraduate student, put her coffee mug down, and stared anxiously at the intervening wall.

Beetle's eye view, thought William, experiencing it for several seconds. Then he snapped back to Stable View and backed out, making for the staircase at the end of the corridor. Stop mucking about, he told himself, unaware that he was doing so out loud, and in one of Kenneth Williams' more camp voices. Get up them stairs.

Resisting the temptation to leap the entire flight in a single bound like Superman, he Stable Speeded up each step, noting as usual that the smoothness of Stable View travel made him feel paradoxically seasick.

Need to work on the head-bounce. How much *does* your head bounce, going upstairs? How can we just run upstairs like that anyway without all the bouncing and changing non-stable viewing making us trip up all the time? Obviously some kind of compensatory balance-mechanism; interesting, thought William, immediately losing interest. Carefully he manoeuvred himself into the back bedroom.

'Wake up, Lewis!' he shouted happily. All appeared stable and coherent.

The bathroom was still the vaguest. Curves were so difficult. The toilet dodged sitting on.

'Highly inconvenient,' William admonished it. In the front bedroom he sat down, as it were, on the bed. How tidy it all was! The wardrobe wouldn't open, would be empty if it did. Whereas the real thing, William thought, wouldn't actually close, so crammed was it with almost every item he had ever owned, right down to a pair of clogs he'd dyed silver and clumped about quite nimbly on in 1971. As yet there was no place in his image-house for things that touched other things; wads, piles, stacks, even one chair slightly behind another, they were all out.

It was a bit eery, thought William, the way you could see into all these corners. In real life there's always something in the way. It was rather like getting out into flat open country and realising how much sky there is when there's no houses or trees about; sky that meets the horizon all around, not only as vaulted roof but seamless wall. Here, too, in his image-house, emptiness somehow implied constriction. I suppose you can forget the limits, thought William, if you can't see where they are, no wonder I'm so untidy myself, and look at gypsies, living on rubbish dumps, and tourists dropping litter . . . where was I? Ah yes. Grand finale time. So remember the head-flex head-flex head-flex –

Revolving on his stool and ducking neatly at just the right moment, William turned himself completely in a circle, noting bed, window, wardrobe, chest of drawers, and bed again in slow smooth progression.

Tricky but superb. Hah hah hah hah hah! William thought he thought. Tomorrow the world!

Next door Julia, hearing further wild laughter, looked strainedly up from her recording electrodes. This was quite as bad as the groans, she thought. And last week there had been a crash: loud groaning, crash, a long silence and then more groans, to be precise. She stood up, irresolute. I really mustn't do this, she thought, picking up the glass someone had left on the windowsill and applying its rim to the party wall. It's spying, I really mustn't. She bent, and pressed her ear to the glass. She held her breath.

William had remembered head-bounce, and was considering recreating it using Rapid Unipolar Displacement. The trouble was, he realised, that head-bounce was one of the many everyday things that you didn't actually notice until you thought about it, and then just thinking about it wasn't enough, you still had to look for it consciously despite having done it or used it unconsciously for years; because surely I don't bounce this much, do I? Or is it everything else that seems to bounce, while I seem to keep myself still?

Already he was noting the sudden internal-rise sensation that heralded nausea.

Yes, but look at pigeons, thought William, applying himself to back-and-forth rather than up-and-down, look at the way their heads jerk about, you'd think they'd get a headache, you'd think they'd get neck-ache at least. Or chickens.

Bwak bwak bwak, thought William, trying for a chicken's-eye view.

Julia could hardly believe her ears. She told her friend from the physiology department all about it at lunch in the central cafeteria.

'And now he's started making *animal* noises,' she finished darkly.

'Animal noises? What, farmyard?'

There was a pause.

'No,' said Julia faintly, 'poultry.' For some moments neither could speak for laughter.

'And you still haven't seen him?' asked Rachel, still exploding now and then.

'No,' Julia sighed, and put her glasses back on. 'It's – Frederick. My professor. You know. Being a psychopath.'

Rachel looked serious. 'He can't keep you prisoner, you know.'

'Well, he sort of can, actually. I mean, I had another go yesterday, I said, Ah, I'd really like a coffee *now* Frederick if you wouldn't mind, because all the others tend to break about now and it would be so helpful to me to talk things over sort of thing. *But.*' She shrugged.

'He said no?'

'Yes, I'm afraid I'm not ready yet, he says. So what can I say, I can't say, Well I'm off, sorry. Not over *coffee*. I'd feel so childish for one thing.'

'It's him who's being childish.'

'That's what I keep telling myself.'

'You should go somewhere else.'

'I should've got a First.'

Pause.

'Too many parties.'

'Maybe.' In this particular old friend's eyes Julia was, she knew, rather a romantic figure, the gifted, careless, heroine of several convoluted love affairs. Looking back it occurred to Julia that this interpretation of her own past was not, after all, so very far from the truth. Though it had felt at the time more like perplexity and mere bad management than glamour, and Rachel's slightly starstruck avidity fraudulently come by as well as an embarrassment.

What had happened, wondered Julia, to make her own memories look like Rachel's version of them? The present has altered them, she thought. My life's like Rachel's now, all chaste and studious. And without thinking about it at all she said aloud, 'Oh, did I tell you? Henry rang last week.'

'No!' Rachel sounded just like the old days.

'Mm. Making an absolute mint, it seems.'

'And are you – going to see him again?'

'Might do. I don't know,' Julia shrugged. 'I've got a lot on at the moment.'

'What, the strabismus?'

'Yes – '

Here Julia described, for a minute or two, the paper she was working on as Professor Fern's research assistant, using terms impenetrable to outsiders, linking abstruse descriptive neologisms to others with what might, to a non-scientific laity, be considered a surprising choice of prefixes and conjunctions; demonstrated the perhaps unfortunate link between the subtlest, the most rigorous of scientific thought and completely uncontrollable linguistics; spoke, in short, in the particular specialised jargon not only of her kind but of her department, her floor, her corridor, even her own cramped office-cum-laboratory.

Rachel, who occupied a different laboratory in an adjoining building, was fluent in the basic language, but stumbled here and there over the regional dialect words.

'What? hemianotropia? I thought you said – '

'I *did* – '

All about them, other voices, other disciplines spoke the infinite tongues of modern science. Two tables down the man who had glued weightless slivers of mirror onto each wing of a certain South American butterfly, the better to film and annotate the complexities of its flight path, described his findings, in terms of the utmost Physiology, to several rapt admiring juniors; over by the window the young woman whose interminable proceedings with various yeasts had recently led to the synthesis of a new and significant immuno-suppressive, spoke gently to a friend in Hydrobotanical; while to Julia's immediate right the man who had spent the last two years of his life trying to discover exactly at what age babies prone to squint begin to do so, was able to describe his mysteriously conflicting data without once mentioning age, babies, or even squints, though the frustrations inherent in attempting to cajole and eye-patch dozens of otherwise perfectly healthy toddlers may well have influenced him here to some extent.

Surroundings were not plush. The fine scientific minds ate their school-dinner lunches from formica tables, beneath strip lighting. Their laboratories all needed cleaning and decorating; a distinguished visiting Scandinavian professor of neurophysiology had sprained his ankle on a curl of linoleum only a week earlier, while the neuro-opthalmologists had lately been forced to squeeze themselves onto two floors, the better to accommodate a band of animal behaviourists whose own department, which to the uninitiated had looked rather like an old-fashioned wooden Scout hut, had unfortunately collapsed the previous winter, damaging several years' worth of data and crushing to death twenty-five experimental hibernating snails.

Julia fell silent. She watched Rachel spearing chips.

'I did see the back of his head once,' she said at last.

'Who, Poultry Man?'

'Yes, going in to see that hairy one, Gerry I think his name is.'

'Radio Man.'

'Mm. He was listening to You and Yours today. So cosy. I can just see him knitting in there.'

'Well, if you're working on hibernation – '

'Yes, you feel he's really got into his subject.'

'Want a pud?'

Julia checked her watch. 'Oh, no thanks.'

'Is he in this afternoon?'

'Yes. And all evening.'

Rachel sighed and tutted. 'Good luck.'

'Thanks,' said Julia, picking up her books and papers quite happily. But as she crossed the road to the laboratory buildings her mood fell again. She was especially oppressed by a recent notion that she herself was partly to blame for some of the professor's behavioural lapses, by being just that little bit too ordinary, when she'd gone all out to convince him, during those fervent last-minute interviews, that despite her degree she really was exceptional; and though she had at the time by some fluke (she told herself gloomily) succeeded, wasn't he now quite justifiably infuriated at finding himself hoodwinked, and lumbered with an Upper Second mind?

Look, he'd just say so, rude old bugger, thought Julia firmly. And anyway, hadn't he come across as Kindly Old Eccentric? It serves us both right.

She pushed open the great glass doors. A few minutes more, and then Frederick, possibly a six- or seven-hour Frederick stint. Julia climbed the stairs slowly, trying to establish whether she had anything nice to look forward to or not. But all she could come up with was the prospect of dinner with Henry one evening the following week, Henry who persistently cast himself these days as doggedly faithful ex-lover, though she had only dated him once or twice anyway, and even then only to cause pain to somebody else.

Bet he'd run a mile if I laid a finger on him, thought Julia, not that I'd want to anyway, I'm not that desperate, am I?

And she rememberd telling Rachel that she hadn't decided yet whether or not to see Henry again, pretending her life was as full of choices as ever. That was depressing, certainly. She had never needed to lie to Rachel before. How long could a bad patch last, Julia wondered, and still be a patch and not the whole thing? Reaching her floor she felt a sudden swoop of panic. Everything is wrong, she thought, clutching the iron bannister with one hand, everything is dreadful and getting worse all the time. For a dreadful dizzy moment she was alone with the truth, but then other truths rushed to their usual action-stations: impossible to give up now, too much waste of time and trying, you've nothing else lined up, you can't let Frederick win, Frederick is your own fault anyway, you should have got a First. And something nice might happen soon.

But I don't suppose it will, thought Julia, starting off down the corridor.

She thought it very clearly, in the hope of tweaking fate into getting a move on at proving her wrong.

'But I don't suppose it will.'

Three

Rita put drops in her eyes to make the whites look blue, and dyed her hair all sorts of different colours. She was very slender, (scrawny, Binnie thought) and so went in for trousers, even tight pale blue jeans sometimes, though this was against the rules. Whereas Binnie's own round tidy perm still resembled the style of the young Queen Elizabeth, as it had since 1955. In short, Rita was not the sort of person Binnie would have spoken to at all, under normal circumstances. As it was, nearly a fortnight had passed before she realised why Rita looked so familiar.

'Do you – live in Orchard Close?'

Of course she did; had done for years. Half a street from Binnie herself, but there had been no call for them to speak, until Binnie had started as a care assistant at the Home as well.

'Two minutes in this place,' said Rita, narrowing her eyes as she tried to light a cigarette at the Aga hotplate, 'and you want to rush out and buy twenty Capstan Full Strength and a bottle of gin.'

The trouble was that once Binnie had realised who Rita was she had also remembered hearing all sorts of things about her: how her husband had beaten her up on their wedding night and then said, 'Fancy a cup of tea?' while she still lay on the floor bleeding, and how sometimes he wouldn't speak for a whole week, wouldn't even look at her, just turned his head away whenever she came in; and how at last but all of a sudden he'd run after Rita with an axe, a real wood-chopping axe he'd evidently bought for the purpose because they'd got all central heating throughout; how he'd chased her round the house jumping and whooping like a Red Indian and bashing the axe into doorways.

No one had heard, or called the police. Rita hadn't called them either, though clearly she had told someone, who'd told someone else; because after he'd made lots of holes in the woodwork he'd run off into the night laughing like something out of a horror film. 'And I've never set eyes on him since,' said Rita, explaining all this one quiet afternoon.

Binnie had been very pleased. Quite apart from it being an entrancing story it was such a relief being officially in the know. Rita's previous references to her husband had made him out to be just ordinarily tiresome, insisting on Great Yarmouth year after year and always turning the bathroom taps off too hard. It had been uncomfortable, knowing about the axe-waving as well.

Once or twice, watching Rita leave work a little early for a date, seeing her swinging up the drive to some waiting car with her dyed hair bouncing and lashings of scent on, Binnie had remembered the axe-man and found herself thinking unpleasantly sneering thoughts: Well she can't be that bright then, marrying a nutcase, and, No one's ever laid a hand on *me*.

'Still, he keeps the payments up all right,' said Rita flatly, 'd'you want another cup?'

It was knowing her secret, Binnie thought now; if you knew someone's secret everything they said that didn't refer to it, everything else they said, was going to sound false somehow; you were going to eye them up from behind your net curtains and feel scornful, you just couldn't help it.

Binnie often felt watched herself, going up Orchard Close to the village, and hurried along always looking straight ahead as if she had a train to catch or something important on her mind.

Once, years ago, she had told her husband about how she felt when she went up the Close and he had said that it wasn't shyness at all really, but vanity, and that everyone had better things to do than stand about looking at her all day.

It's whether they know your secrets, she mentally told him now, coming up with the answer at last. And I suppose they do, or I wouldn't feel them looking so much, would I? What would it feel like if I was imagining it, how would it be different?

Thinking about the years she had been walking up and down Orchard Close reminded her of something.

'Ooh, did you know Jean Shone's moving?'

'Old Jean! No!'

'Told me yesterday, she's on the market, I don't want to go, she says, all my children grew up here, but the house feels so big, and what with the rates and everything, she says – '

'And repairs, I know I have terrible trouble – '

'She's looking for something smaller, in the village or somewhere.'

Rita shook her wild head, blonde this month. 'They're all going, the old crowd.'

'There's hardly anyone left,' Binnie agreed, 'who moved in first off.'

'It's you and me, practically. Gor, that was a time!'

Binnie smiled politely, though her memories of those early days were, she suspected, very different from Rita's.

Jean Shone had appeared on the front doorstep when the Solways were moving in, all those years ago, wading through the mud in her wellingtons and carrying a full pot of tea. She had beamed and told the Solways they were welcome, and Binnie, rather awkward in the face of this show of friendly self-confidence, had thanked her with smiles that were, perhaps, a little closed and forbidding; certainly friendship had hardly prospered from the start.

'Terrible cup of tea,' Binnie had remarked, *sotto voce*, when Mrs Shone had gone. Besides, the Shones had turned out to have three noisy and ill-disciplined little children and a hi-fi set, and a tendency to very late-night parties, attended by most of the other younger and less respectable couples in and around Orchard Close; including the very young Rita, remembered Binnie, with her newly-married future axe-man.

Every third or fourth Saturday night, when the Shones' half of the semi would vibrate to Nat King Cole and Helen Shapiro, glass-chinks and yells of laughter, Binnie would lie fiercely awake over in her half, rigid with rage. Eric claimed not to be bothered by the noise, and insisted that if he looked worn and haggard every third or fourth Sunday morning it was because of Binnie complaining and bouncing about beside him, hissing 'Listen to *that*!' every five minutes.

Once Binnie, clad only in nightwear and a frilly nylon curler cap, had knocked angrily on the Shones' front door at three o'clock in the morning, and demanded consideration, whereupon Mr Shone and several of his mates had staggered beerily round her in a circle, sniggering in a very insulting way. Later that morning little William Solway had voluntarily done a full hour's particularly heavy-handed piano practice, and ten years of unremitting conflict had followed.

Early one summer evening as William played football against the closed doors of the garage, Mr Shone, a hefty blue-chinned individual whose dense chest hair made him look like a man in a black furry T-shirt, had swung himself belligerently over the new garden fence and spoken very roughly, ordering William to lay off. Binnie, indignantly hammering on the Shones' front door once more, had been told that the eldest Shone child had feverish tonsilitis, which would have been enough to baulk her had not Mr Shone then gone on to remark that William was a little bleeder.

A week or so after this the Solways had happened to rearrange their front-room furniture, and happened in doing so to place their piano right against the party wall.

Later that year Binnie, out shopping in the village, had come across Jean Shone, who was standing outside Liptons with two friends of hers, one of whom might even have been Rita, Binnie couldn't be quite certain looking back; anyway Binnie had hurried by as usual pretending not to notice anyone or anything in particular and just as she passed them all three younger women had burst out laughing.

Binnie had been depressed about this for several weeks. Mrs Shone had gained further ground when, catching Binnie in the back garden as both women were putting out their washing, she had abruptly and loudly announced that

Binnie's treatment of the Solways' dog, which was kept most mornings tied by a fairly long rope to the wash-pole, was making the Shones' lives a misery. The little Shones especially, said Mrs Shone, could hardly bear to witness such cruelty.

Almost all Binnie could do by way of reply to this new offensive was helplessly to make the Solways' lives equally miserable in return. Also she had to go on relentlessly tying the dog up, for months, long after it had outgrown the original puppyish and suicidal car-chasing habits that had prompted her to tie it up in the first place, grimly untangling its legs from the rope every half-hour or so and trying to close her ears to its wretched cries of loneliness and boredom: all this was Jean Shone's fault.

At the end of this decade, however, Mrs Shone became pregnant again. This in itself was scarcely pacifying, since the last baby had been a day-and-night screamer, and Mrs Shone, whatever her views on canine suffering, had often been obliged to park the child, strapped bawling in its pram, in her back garden, where for some time it had added its wails to those of the captive dog.

But the fourth baby was a quiet child. After its birth Mrs Shone, noted though overtly ignored in the High Street or putting out or taking in her washing, had appeared rather wan and subdued, and more than once outright scruffy. Then one day, in the spring, Binnie, straightening up from the weeding, had looked over the fence at the occupied pram and seen, as the baby kicked its little legs in the air, an indubitable flash, as of metal.

Binnie felt a corresponding flash in her heart, of horror and pity, and as she came closer and watched for the metallic shine to repeat itself, Mrs Shone came out, and saw her.

'Hallo,' said Binnie, for the first time in years. Mrs Shone, after a moment's hesitation, nodded in reply.

'How – is he?' asked Binnie, going right up to the fence. It was a club-foot.

'Poor little mite,' said Binnie. 'Hasn't he got a lovely smile!'

Even this might not, in itself, have been enough to end hostilities but presently, after a year or so's increasingly audible rows, it became known throughout the entire housing estate that Mr Shone had found himself another woman, and that he was leaving Mrs Shone with the house and the children, but intended taking the family car. He took the new stereo as well.

Not long after this the Solways decided to move their front room furniture back to its original position, just by way of a change; and not long after that Jean popped round to ask the Solways' advice when the back boiler wouldn't rake clear; and when Jean, unasked, took Binnie's washing in for her one unexpectedly wet Monday Binnie, going across to thank her and collect the washing, had walked past the front door and gone round the side to the kitchen, and several years of peaceful friendship had followed.

'But now there's only me and Jason, you see,' said Jean, calling round with her latest news, 'and the place just feels so big.'

Binnie had nodded sadly. At night, by the gas fire, she too had felt the weight of the rooms upstairs, the two empty bedrooms enclosing cold and silence above her head.

'Oh I don't want to go, my kids all grew up here, you know what I mean?'

'Yes . . .' And the houses still looked so new, Binnie had thought. They hardly looked old enough to have contained whole lives. Sometimes it hardly seemed a week or so since those Sunday afternoon picnics when she and Eric and young William had driven over – no, caught two connecting buses – to check on their new house's progress.

They were the first, she and Eric, in all her family or his, to be buying their own house. And as if that wasn't enough in itself it was to be a sparkling brand-new architect-designed countryside home; she could see the brochure still if she closed her eyes, *Your Dream Home Come True* in a sort of rainbow over the smart pointy-toed young couple wandering embraced and smiling in the foreground. Looking at them you could tell they'd never had to struggle with the complex messes other people always seemed to leave behind, the blackish furry grease behind the cooker after years of someone else's fry-ups, the blurred shape on the wallpaper behind the bed where someone else had leant his brilliantined head during his first cigarette or his early cup to tea; no pocked or curling lino, no sinister spongy layers of carpet. No mice.

How healthy their lives, that happy couple! How easily made clean!

She and Eric too, Binnie had vaguely imagined then, would take on some of that freshness when their own lives were free of the muddles other people left behind. And they would be living in the country, in what had, until the previous year, been an actual Kentish hopfield.

She had so enjoyed these early visits, watching their lives being built. They had waded along the foundations, stood on rough floors of concrete imagining walls. Once she had run on in front, pretending to open an imaginary front door; Eric had pretended not to notice. Sudden roof timbers, interlocking like a tiny cathedral; the exciting staircase, leading nowhere; the new roof's darkness; the dumpy breeze blocks, curtaining off space, front room, kitchen, downstairs cloaks; her sadness when the windows went in, tame ordinary windows, instead of the cheerful gape of frames. The place looked so serious suddenly, a real building, no longer the half-built playground Wendy-house full of sly jutting twists of wire or unexplained holes; she had even tried saying something along these lines to Eric, so really after all it must have been a very long time ago, thought Binnie now.

And moving-in day: the shock of it. The house seemed to have shrunk several sizes what with all the plaster and the wallpaper and what was clearly and infuriatingly two different shades of off-white tiling in the bathroom. The kitchen door-handle had come off in her hand, and in the new stiff cupboard under the sink she had come across a fat little bag of plaster, abandoned there; a rounded little bag, slackly curved against the water pipes at the back. Kneeling in her flowered apron she had leant forwards to touch its yielding powdery softness, and met rock instead, the dampened bag had set solid, like an animal somehow fossilised whole. Impossible to explain the noise she had made, not the sort of womanly little shriek that could have been mainly laughter, but a real deep pan-human scream, at the bag's small rounded shoulders all turned to stone.

'Caught my finger,' she had breathlessly explained to Eric, who'd come bursting in at her yell, he'd been furious, she'd made him drop the cutlery canteen all over the parquet, causing the first in that series of dents and pockmarks long since hidden beneath the wall-to-wall. She'd upset William too, screaming like that; he'd looked quite pale all afternoon, she remembered.

And it was just after all that, that Jean Shone came round with her teapot, no wonder I was flustered . . .

'We're the original inhabitants, we are,' said Rita suddenly, breaking in.

'What, sorry?'

'Miles away. I said, we're the last original inhabitants, that place. You and me.'

'Oh yes, I suppose so.'

Getting on for thirty years. Funny how many things had changed, and what things. Dogs, for instance. First, they'd just run wild, you opened the back door to let the dog out, and it would take itself for a walk, or join up with its mates; but nowadays dogs had got like Victorian maidens, you never saw one unchaperoned, they were always being walked up the Close or into the Avenue, with collars and leads on. Only council estate dogs roamed free these days.

And the hops: the hops had finally stopped trying. How far back? At first every spare patch of ground had grown them, poor innocent young hop-plants, or so they had seemed to Binnie, that had popped up gaily expecting support, found none, and collapsed into debased and stateless crawlers, clinging to obviously temporary brick-piles or lying broken under every passing builder's barrow or every other housewife's passing pram.

Eric had made quite a bonfire of them in the newly enclosed and suddenly tiny back garden, but for years afterwards the occasional spindly refugee had managed to flower among the runner beans or hide behind the clematis. Not for a long time now though, thought Binnie. Original inhabitants. Would Rita remember them? By now, however, Binnie knew better than to ask.

'She's got her eye on one of the terraces in Station Road,' said Binnie. 'Jean Shone. Said she'd like the noise, and there'd always be someone about.'

But the idea of it had rather upset her. She saw Jean

turning by fast degrees into an old village lady, treading slowly about the High Street in her clean old lady's shoes or sitting looking out of her front-room window. She almost looked the part already, with her prematurely white hair and worn pale face. Binnie had had a sudden clear memory, of Jean in her scandalous prime, rakish in a tight pink party frock; not so very long ago.

'I'm really going to miss her,' said Binnie now to Rita.

'What old Jean? Yeah. All the old crowd's going.'

A bell rang.

'It's that Edith,' said Rita, checking. 'I'm gonna *get* her a flaming taxi one a these days. See what happens.'

'She wouldn't know where to ask for. Anyway he wouldn't take her, the taxi driver. Not in her nightie. They don't take you like that.'

'It's heaven she wants to go to,' said Rita, carrying her cup to the sink. 'I'd let her go, myself.'

It was clear from the way she said this that she had forgotten hearing a gentler pitched version of it from Binnie herself about a week earlier; so Binnie pretended to have forgotten as well, smiling and shaking her head.

'Well you got to laugh in this place,' said Rita, drying her hands on a tea towel, 'or you'd cry, you doing the supper trays?'

The bell rang again.

'All right all right. See you.' She clopped away in her Dr Scholls.

Binnie sat still for a few moments more. What would Rita say, when she'd lost her suitcase? Perhaps whatever it was she'd been about to say just before the man jumped yelling over the threshold, just before she saw the whirling axe.

'Shepherd's pie all right?'

Yes, that would flummox and bore them, fifty years hence.

Rita now could bend with Edith, cheerfully shouting, 'Where to, Edith? Off again, Edith?' and one day women not yet born might use just the same tones on her.

'Ooh yes please, Rita!'

'Not again, Rita!'

Shepherd's pie all right?

She would sound bored and casual, thought Binnie, half-grinning as she cleared the table. Whereas I'll sound excited, talking to my darling.

To step back into that memory, and stay there, that would be worth growing old and silly for. She took down the pile of formica trays, and began setting them with cutlery and a large lacy paper doily each.

But of course that's wrong, she remembered. You lose the suitcase, you just keep reading out the label.

This thought somehow made the kitchen seem terribly quiet, so presently she crossed it and put the radio on, and was able to stop thinking altogether.

Four

The house was in darkness when William let himself in. He slammed the door and clumped about noisily in the passageway, in case Lewis was being uninhibited in the front room, but when he stood still all was quiet.

Out, then. He's out all the time these days, thought William fretfully. He carried the mail through into the kitchen, but it was all for Lewis apart from the electricity bill. Lewis's looked quite interesting as well: two handwritten ones. William held these up to the light, trying to read the postmarks, but both were fragmented and illegible. He flattened the back of each envelope, and through one was just able to trace out a line: 'after all when we were in'

In what? thought William, squinting, but unable to make out anything more. In love? In Paris? In bed?

In Wolverhampton, he told himself stoutly. In hospital. In prison. He sniggered, and the sound awoke him. Pawing Lewis's mail: pathetic. He put the letters down and offered himself a cup of tea.

Don't mind if I do. He picked the kettle up and after some manoeuvring managed to work its spout into position under the tap. Surprising how brackish the water was, he thought, peering into the crowded sink, and he remembered scraping a piece of toast over it the day before. Shouldn't it have been Maisie's day today? Or perhaps it wasn't Friday after all.

He rinsed out a mug, wiping off the wet brown ring inside it with his fingers. What day was it then? Frowning he dropped in a teabag. It wasn't yesterday Lewis had been crying over Coronation Street, that had been the day before, so two days ago was either Monday or Wednesday. So I still don't know, thought William, losing interest.

He squatted in front of the fridge, holding things in with one hand while scouting for the milk. That gravy boat still there then, little green islands in it now. Something shrouded in bacofoil still there. Same three bits of old cheese, each drying into a yellowish transparency and looking just like the dead skin you get on your heels, thought William, running a finger along one hard shrunken edge.

As he did so he suddenly remembered using his father's toenail clippers, long ago, to bite off satisfyingly large wedges of his own dead old-cheddar heels, result of over-roomy football boots; a bathtime memory so vivid that for a moment he was sitting not in his own grown-up Hackney kitchen but in the damp cooling bathroom of his parents' house, nearly fifteen and so unendurably irritated by the sound of his parents breathing in the front room that long dreamy baths were the only option, once homework was done.

I'd forgotten the claustrophobia, thought William, standing up and finding a bottle of milk in one hand. You forget how strong they were, or seemed.

He held the bottle to his nose and sniffed hard. Risk it? Spooning up the drowned teabag he had a go at throwing in into the rubbish bin from here, and missed; but he pretended not to have noticed, and left it lying prone on the lino while he sat at the table, trying to blow the small fatty blobs floating in his tea over to the far side of the mug.

So, Lewis was out there having a good time somewhere. Everyone was out there having a good time, or staying in and being romantic; presently William imagined himself picking up the telephone and, quite casually really, calling Laura; went into it in some detail for several seconds before he realised what he was doing and told himself sharply to lay off.

It was dismal but there was nothing for it: he took the mug upstairs and went to bed.

But as soon as he fell asleep he dreamt of tripping up, and woke abruptly, saving himself; and recognised almost immediately that somehow he lay, not in his own real-life bedroom, but in his vibrant lime-green image of it; knew, sweating with dread, that if he opened his eyes he wouldn't see his real stuffed and gaping wardrobe at the foot of the bed, but its blank empty facsimile; which meant that if he lifted up his own real hand, yes, like this, and took a look, he would see not his own familiar fingers but . . .

In his dream William screamed, and tried to run, but his outsize football boots held him fast. So he snapped on Stable Speed, leapt laughing into the air like Superman, and flew away instead.

A mile or so to William's north-west, where the corner shops were Greek rather than Asian and the small terraced houses cost half as much again, Julia was nearly home, close on midnight. Frederick had been in one of his teasing moods; had discovered some basic flaw in last week's runthroughs, and thought it would be useful for her to find the fault out for herself, by doing the whole lot all over again while he watched.

Julia's only recourse had been to work as slowly as possible, to avoid, she had explained, any possibility of repeating her mistake, and presently Frederick had grown most satisfyingly bored, to judge by the crescendo of small noises he had made: sharp nasal breathings-out like a shy person laughing, creaks as he swung his swivel chair round in circles, nail-biting noises, interspersed with short explosive spitting-out noises and the brisk damp flickerings made by someone violently rubbing at his ears with his bunched fingertips.

After this he had prowled around the office touching things and lining up already perfectly squared-off piles of papers, and humming to himself. It was the hum that gave him away, Julia thought: a hum like that meant battle joined. She had fought back by stopping work altogether and taking her handbag to the ladies room for twenty minutes, where she had sat eating a Mars bar and reading a very old copy of *Good Housekeeping*, borrowed that morning from the waiting room, just in case.

Frederick had disappeared by the time she got back but even working at normal speed had kept her going until nearly ten, when she had eaten a bag of small cushion-shaped crunchy things from the machine in the hallway and later, driven by hunger, a pot of someone else's apricot yoghurt, stolen from the coffee-room fridge. She would buy a replacement on the way to work tomorrow, she told herself without much conviction, swallowing the stuff down hastily in case Frederick came back and caught her, spoon in hand.

All in all, thought Julia, sliding her key into her own front door at last, things could've been worse; the basic flaw had turned out to be something anyone other than Frederick would have warned her about anyway, but that was par for the course and besides he'd been well seen off. Though the long-hours-in-the-ladies stunt might well turn out to be counter-productive in the end; it wouldn't do to use it too often.

'Evie?'

The kitchen light was on, but the room was empty and extremely clean and neat, nothing even left to drain. The place smelt faintly, of Anais Anais. One of the chairs wore a brownish tweed overcoat round its shoulders. Julia ran a finger over the collar. It was his all right.

'Oh dear,' said Julia softly, sounding like someone a little bored and dismayed, as in, 'Oh dear, Evie's got back with Whathisname again, what a nuisance'; in fact her heart was pounding and her stomach had dizzily missed a step, but Julia was ashamed of all this evidence and instantly determined to rule it inadmissible.

'Oh dear . . .'

Oh Christ, Julia's body might have thought had Julia quite let it, It's me really on my own again now, no more jolly nights out with Evie and Philly and Jo, oh all alone again listening to her and him splashing in the bath together and being extra quiet in her room on account of me, and me in my bed all alone –

'Oh dear,' said Julia again, managing to sound almost sarcastic. She had been covering this dreadful lament with other less painful thoughts, still true but diversionary; as when, a child at the cinema, she had stuffed her fingers in her ears during the frightening bits, and determinedly hummed a cheery tune over the screams and the terrifying scream-music:

Well, really Evie's being rather a bore to bother with Mr Dull yet again, she's obviously made all the running, I give it three months before we're all back to square one again, when I think of the hours I put in, all that sympathetic listening and listening and making helpful tactical suggestions and taking her out shopping and talking for hours about what sort of new hairdo she should go for –

All this while Julia was making herself some Horlicks, yanking the fridge door open, snatching up the carton, bashing the milk pan down on the hob.

'I'm actually quite angry with her,' Julia told herself, noticing all this violence, and for a moment, these things being perfectly easy to arrange, she felt really lightheaded with anger, and had to take some slow deep breaths to calm herself down.

'I mean, she didn't even mention it to me, and I feel she's, you know, made rather a fool of me in a way,' she imagined herself wryly telling someone. And she stirred her Horlicks furiously, ting ting ting ting ting, wearing a particularly wry smile as if in demonstration.

But in bed later nothing, no mental thumbs-in-ears, no frantic humming, could quite shut out the screams and their incidental music.

I could cope with work, with Frederick, with there being no men in London, not one, unless you count that Henry, I could do it all, but not with this as well, thought Julia, still awake at nearly two and not even trying to read.

Should I find somewhere else to live?

She thought of the dismal boring struggle this would entail. Was it worth all that to get away from Evie, just because Evie was making her feel like Rachel? It was hardly

Evie's fault if she was better-looking and so stylish, and her increasingly frequent bits of advice on what Julia ought or ought not to wear were just friendly, kindly meant and well worth taking on the whole. It's ridiculous to try to blame her in any way for my being so Rachel-ish.

But I used to tell Rachel what to wear, didn't I?

Oh, the past! Three years of being the only nice-looking girl, nearly the only woman, in an entire university department! Perhaps it's spoiled me for life, thought Julia, not for the first time.

Her arms felt jumpy with the desire to hold someone. They wanted to enfold. She could feel them longing, almost as if they were separate and speaking to her.

'Oh,' sighed Julia, helplessly hearing them.

Worse was the other voice, of which she was ashamedly a little ashamed, perplexed by; the small poignant voice of sexual desire, not aggressive or bullying, as she had read male Furies were, but wistful, apologetic, reproachful.

I'm a space, said the voice, sad as her arms. I'm a space, fill me.

It didn't want babies, this voice, thought Julia, examining it. It didn't care about meaningful relationships or proper homes of loving families. It wasn't asking much. It was a pleading voice.

'I'm a space: fill me.'

'Oh shut up!' groaned Julia aloud, turning onto her stomach and pressing her face into the pillow.

Bloody Evie. I'm sorry Evie. But I could cope when you were in the same boat. And now it's all worse worse worse –

Julia turned onto her back again, where the voice was always at its most insistent, and began resignedly to do what she could about it.

Five

Eric had fallen asleep on the sofa, and Binnie had kept the television on, not so much to watch it as to sit in front of its liveliness, as if it were a real coal fire.

Every now and then she looked up from the particularly dull stretch of left back she was working on to see people piling into cars, or rushing out of them leaving all the doors open. It was somehow glamorous to leave all the doors open, Binnie could see that.

So if I see a real policeman jump out of his car leaving the door open, she thought, I'll know where he's got it from, and what he'd like to be like.

Thinking this Binnie had a sudden very clear memory of herself during the war, looking out of the Nissen hut window at another WAAF, a blonde girl from Rayleigh, who'd had a row with her fiancé and been very quiet all day, and who'd now gone off outside to wander about in the corner of untended ground behind the hut, brushing her hair off her forehead with the back of her hand and pulling the heads off dog-daisies, tearing at the petals, scattering them in the deep grass at her feet.

Now why on earth should I remember her? Binnie thought back, came upon car doors, and saw a connection.

It would be the same sort of embarrassment, knowing where the policeman got his style from and seeing that blonde girl yanking at the daisies. I'd seen what a pretty picture she felt she was, I'd thought, Bet she tells him afterwards, when they've made it up.

'Oh darling, I was so upset, I went wandering into the meadow (well, she wouldn't say scruffy little corner, would she?), I went wandering into the meadow behind the hut and I pulled at the flowers – '

So he'd see the nice romantic picture as well, his pretty true-love flushed among the petals; himself as absent hero too.

Or perhaps he had seen through it, felt that special sort of shame, the kind you ignore when you want to go on being with someone. Maybe that was the call-sign then, thought Binnie, and a little round weight of sadness and regret formed itself in the usual place, just below her waistband.

It wasn't just the blonde girl, it was more complicated; not just my memory of her, but my memory of imagining her boyfriend; she matched up with the policeman's car doors, but he matched up with –

How many more rows of this anyway? Binnie asked herself just in time. Have I lost count?

She shook the knitting pattern free from her bag and stared at it for a minute or so, though without actually reading it.

'Eh?' asked Binnie aloud, giving the pattern a little shake. This somehow enabled her to focus her eyes on it, and remember which bit she was checking on. She checked, counting. Damn. Done too many.

'Damn damn damn,' said Binnie softly to herself, and

from the sofa where he lay Eric gulped as if in reply, startled, and awoke.

'Mwah!'

'Had your forty winks,' said Binnie sharply, her eyes on her knitting.

Eric rubbed at his eyes under his glasses, and nodded over at the television.

'What's all this?' he asked hopefully, but Binnie only shrugged, and ripped out another row. All that she had been thinking of had slipped away and disappeared, but the little round weight of unhappiness had got left behind.

'No idea,' she sniffed. 'Load of rubbish.'

Right you are, thought Eric, have it your own way.

'Think I'll just take a turn then,' he said heartily, getting up.

'Thirty-two, thirty-three,' said Binnie warningly.

Outside the air was damp and fresh with next door's cypress hedge. Eric put his hands in his pockets and walked along quite slowly, looking at the curtained windows as he passed. The houses all looked so nice in the dark, cosy and glowing. He checked his watch, and found he had timed it just right.

At the corner he sat down on the low wall by the bus stop and took the cigarette packet out of his pocket. There was half a one left from the night before, he knew. He tapped it free; even in the lamplight you could tell which one it was, by the stained filter.

Well bugger all that, thought Eric, putting it in his mouth and getting a match ready. He checked his watch again. Right then; just about now. He struck the match, lit the stub, and had barely taken his first giddying drag when he caught the train's earliest distant thrumming. He leant forward; the track, thirty yards or so away, began to make small humming and clicking noises, anticipatory; the train's muffled roar clarified suddenly as it left the short tunnel three fields back. Eric could have counted the seconds now, five, four, three, two, one, and the train, its golden windows studded with stiff little toytown heads and shoulders, poured itself from there to here, shot piecemeal past a dozen houses, gleamed its red tail-light and withdrew, a fast fade, back into distant thunder. The tracks clicked again, like sighing.

Eric threw the cigarette butt into the gutter and stood up. In his other pocket, the Polos: no need to ask for trouble. He took them out, popped one in, and strolled on.

Six

William awoke very early, feeling obscurely sorry for himself. The house seemed very empty all around him. He turned in bed and switched the radio on, remembering as he did so that it needed new batteries, had done for days. The voices, for an instant strident and authoritative, dwindled quickly into a breathy burbling, as if the studio had suddenly been plunged underwater but with everyone determinedly carrying on as usual, in aqualungs. For a moment William pictured the presenters flippering gently up and down during the interviews and weather reports; but you'd have a lot of trouble with the electrics, he decided, tapping the off-switch.

Could he have an underwater room in the image-house? No reason why not, of course. Reason need not apply there at all.

I could flood the basement completely, for instance. Or I could fill up Lewis's bedroom. I could make it like that Japanese wave-print, make it wash you down the stairs. Underwater graphics, tricky but not impossible: you could swim underwater, no need for oxygen, no need to get wet. I could mock up the whole Pacific, thought William, folding his arms behind his head and giving himself up completely to fantasy.

The house could just be the start. First he'd make it perfect, pictorial rather than diagrammatic. And not just his own house but any house. So you could don the helmet, reach for your keyboard, and travel without moving, through, say, Buckingham Palace, complete in every detail down to the reflected light on the polished floors and each separate crystal drop in the chandeliers; climb upstairs and downstairs, float firmly along corridors or up to the ceiling to peer at the plasterwork, bounce on the beds, skate over the tables, and all without inconveniencing Her Majesty in the slightest; leaving no trace behind; touching, moving, changing nothing; being, in short, a sort of ghost.

The ghost in the machine, thought William, remembering a book Laura had once lent him. A ghost, a little piece of real human mind, travelling through a computerised image of reality, a pure idea at large amongst the applied.

And no need to stay indoors. Why not recreate Paris, empty the Place de la Concorde, swing on the Notre Dame monsters, and climb the Eiffel Tower without using the lift?

I could reproduce the world, thought William, smiling drowsily. Everyone could nip across to Venice during the adverts, or go to watch the sun rise over the Serengeti because it was raining again outside. Sweet controllable dreams.

Leave your body behind, thought William, turning comfortably onto his side. Travel light. Be your own spirit guide.

He snuggled deeper into his pillow. Go anywhere you please, he thought, so long as you don't mind going there on your own.

He kept his eyes closed, and lay very still. But already he knew that once again sleep would elude him.

Julia slept through the alarm, and woke to the sound of the front door slamming. Evie's off early, thought Julia cosily, and then snapped upright, uttered a dazed amalgam of several different swear-words at once, struggled into her clothes, and raced downstairs, pausing only to snatch one of Evie's Coxes from the bowl in the kitchen as she passed.

It was several seconds before she realised why the front door wouldn't open: that Evie, responsible landlady and used to leaving last, habitually double-locked it; that, back on Mr Boring's arm, she would have been in no state to notice Julia's coat still slung over the bannister, or her bicycle still padlocked to the privet hedge outside.

'Evie!' shouted Julia, madly smacking at the door with one hand, 'Evie, help, help!' But of course there was no reply. Julia gave the door a fierce kick, rushed back to the kitchen, scrabbled in the biscuit tin for the back door key, jerked the back door open, and ran outside.

It was a tiny garden, dank and snail-ridden and enclosed on all three sides by tall woven fencing; a fragile drunken sort of fencing, Julia noticed for the first time, propping up or being propped up by a surprisingly large variety of thick but spindly bushes, all covered in enormous spiny thorns and dripping wet.

The only way over that lot, thought Julia wildly, would be using a pole-vault, and for a moment the sudden vivid image of herself, in her nice working skirt and court shoes, shooting shoulders first over a long striped bendy pole, completely diverted her. Then she smacked herself quite hard on the forehead with her palms and ran inside again, raced back up the stairs, and, after a moment's hesitation, opened Evie's bedroom door, and stepped inside.

Very tidy, she noticed at once. Fat little candles everywhere. Flowers by the bed.

Evie's idea, then, not his. And definitely planned. I bet she'll make out otherwise. That Evie. But I'll know.

Feeling almost cheerful Julia wrenched up the sash window, knelt before it, and poked her head out.

Anyone? But the house was at the end of a cul-de-sac; I could be waiting here all day, thought Julia, who had somehow forgotten this and had pictured several helpful smiling unthreatening female passers-by, all conveniently ready to catch Julia's tossed-out key ring to set her free.

Climb down? The downstairs windows were all sealed. But I could definitely, oh Lord, climb down from here, thought Julia, sliding one leg over the sill and wincingly testing the front door's little stone canopy. Suppose it came free from the brickwork though and crashed to the ground, taking me with it? It would cost a fortune to replace as well. Seizing thankfully on this last respectably financial excuse Julia climbed inside again and sat back to consider.

Phone in sick?

No. Not again, not yet. Too late to be convincing anyway.

Phone Evie at work, ask her to come back? No, out of the question. And God!

'Oh my God!' cried Julia aloud. Suppose Evie didn't come back at all tonight, suppose she went home with Mr Dull, and stayed there with him all week! Julia saw herself wan and ragged, scavenging through the swing-bin, scratching tally-marks on the kitchen wall like the Count of Monte Cristo.

Give over, thought Julia, sniggering to herself. All the

same she suddenly felt extremely hungry. Might as well have a proper breakfast, she told herself, going downstairs again, but after all that Horlicks the night before and what had evidently been a very elegant breakfast for two (croissant crumbs, noted Julia scornfully) there was nothing in the fridge but orange juice and a tub of margarine.

At this point Julia's spirits, which had been rather high from suddenly starring in a farce, drooped; she remembered the generally staid and gloomy production she usually played in. Perhaps this morning fitted in with it after all. Imprisoned at home, imprisoned at work, thought Julia and this piece of neatness cheered her enough to prompt her over to the breadbin, where she found a packet of crumpets, nearly whole. Squeezing two of them into the toaster she thought, I'll laugh about this one day.

Which was rather a mistake really, since it was a consolation-line she had been using rather too often lately. The part of Julia that wanted to rest her head on the kitchen table and wail nearly won out at this latest repetition, but the stouthearted side thought fast and came up with Evie's position in all this, her satisfyingly complete in-the-wrongness, and the possible long-term uses this might be put to in the future.

How often have I had to sit through her for instance going on and on about that roast duck that time, everyone laughing and thinking how peculiar I must be and gosh how easygoing good old Evie is putting up with that sort of thing, well! She'll think twice about it now, when I can counter with a dopey-Evie story just as good.

Or was it, after all, another Julia-story? Wouldn't Evie somehow make it so?

'No . . . of course I didn't know . . . our absentminded professor . . . there all day poor love . . . not a *crumb* left in all the house . . . yes, like a sort of guard-dog, ha ha ha . . .'

Julia sighed, and bit into another crumpet. Best not to tell her at all, perhaps. Escape somehow, but keep mum. Just eat all her crumpets for revenge. This reminded Julia of something. She stopped chewing for a moment, concentrating, and came up with office-wear pole-vaulting: not quite what she had been groping after, perhaps, but a pleasant enough diversion all the same.

Fully-clad Olympics, thought Julia, grinning. The men would be all right somehow. Men sprinting in, say, evening dress: they'd look strange perhaps, but sexy rather than comical. Whereas running in skirts, or high-diving in ballgowns, that would surely raise a few smiles. Was it sport that showed up the basic silliness of female clothing, or vice versa?

Oh. Of course.

Julia sat up straight; of course I can get out at the back, easily, she thought. I just get changed, jeans, an old top. Keyring between teeth, piratical; clamber through and over ramshackle fencing, using end stoutly nailed to wall; open front door from outside; get changed back into office things.

So I wasn't helpless at all, thought Julia, carrying her greasy plate to the sink. Not at all, I was just thinking in the wrong clothes.

Seven

Mrs Simmonds was Binnie's favourite, though at first she had been the most frightening. Her mind was almost all in order, but something worse than old age had fastened on her body, drawing the bones into novel curves and outcroppings, and playfully twisting the outer Mrs Simmonds, her skin and flesh, to match the sloppy irresponsible structures underneath.

'Hallo again, ready for your bath?'

'Oh yes please *thank you* dear,' said Mrs Simmonds warmly.

'See, she's not being polite and nice because she has to be, you being the nurse and her all stuck like that,' Binnie had lately remarked to Rita.

'She'd be better off barmy,' Rita had conceded, 'not fair, is it?'

'Got your new soap,' said Binnie now, holding it up. 'Smell.'

She held the cake beneath Mrs Simmonds's nose. Mrs Simmonds inhaled furiously.

'Oh *yum!*'

'This a velcro one? . . . yes . . . here it comes . . .' It was an art, undressing Mrs Simmonds without hurting her.

'No hurry,' said Binnie untruthfully, pausing at a particularly tricky elbow joint. 'I'll just . . . pull it here . . .'

This stage often made Binnie remember her own living bones, made her believe in them and worry about them, the way nature programmes made her believe in pollution and worry about tigers: deeply, for a while.

'There. All right?'

Mrs Simmonds smiled, over the first hurdle and a little breathless.

'Ready?'

'One moment . . . please.'

Binnie waited.

The table beside the bed was covered with photographs: several babies, a couple of colourful weddings, and at the back a row of what Binnie half-consciously thought of as proper photographs, because they were black-and-white; the very young Mrs Simmonds, dreamily in profile and slightly out of focus, which Binnie reached out to tilt on its base a little, so that the poor girl couldn't see her future all twisted on the bed beside her; a First World War soldier also dreaming into the distance, and another wedding, Captain and Mrs Simmonds, staring seriously into the camera, as well they might, thought Binnie, getting up and going over for another closer look.

Yes, there he was; Captain Simmonds, almost hidden behind his tremendous spurting moustache, Captain Simmonds and his great-grandmother, Mrs Simmonds.

Binnie took the yellow duster from her overall pocket and gave the Captain a quick wipe. Ah, but it would have a different feel to it, the other way round. She picked up the dreamy young Mrs Simmonds and rubbed at the silver frame, thinking along well-worn tracks.

Men can always re-marry. Especially after a war. And

look at Mr Pilbeam up the corridor, with his old sepia photograph, the first Mrs P., who'd died of the 'flu. You see her and you think, What a pity, poor girl! Whereas Mrs Simmonds, you don't look at the Captain so much, you look at her, and you think, What a waste! As if she's done nothing since 1917 but hang over his photograph, like a sort of tidy Miss Havisham. Because a man can stay married to the past, as he gets older he can yearn more, not less, he can appreciate the youth, not feel betrayed by it.

And for a moment Binnie stood in Selfridges' millinery department, on a cold Saturday morning in the early spring of 1951, looking at herself in a grey-blue fedora designed for the girl she had suddenly, it seemed, stopped being.

'?'

A small noise from the bed snapped her back to the present.

'Oh sorry, miles away. Right. There. That got too cold?'

'No, no. Just right.'

'There . . . good . . . and the other one – '

'Oh!'

'Sorry, did I – '

'No, um. Please. I was just remembering something.'

'Really?' asked Binnie invitingly, but Mrs Simmonds did not reply, closing her eyes and seeming to drift suddenly into sleep, as she often did.

Poor old thing, thought Binnie, soaping and rinsing carefully. How old she was as well, how properly and nineteenth-century old! Some of the others, though still old enough to be going on with, barely had half a generation on Binnie herself.

It's not just policemen who seem to get younger all the time, thought Binnie, gentle with the towel, it's the old folk as well. Working here you soon get to see how young old people really are.

'But I can see *now*,' said Mrs Simmonds, suddenly opening her eyes and speaking as if without a pause, 'that I was completely wrong.'

'Oh?'

'Yes, it was the flannel, do forgive me, I suddenly remembered the ostler, very Irish face, snub nose sort of thing, saying Top of the morning, it could've been yesterday – '

'Oh yes,' said Binnie.

'Yes,' said Mrs Simmonds sadly. There was another long silence while Binnie patted and powdered everything dry. This was not easy, as Mrs Simmonds seemed to have so much extra skin, and all of it fragile, so you couldn't get up any friction. Gently Binnie lifted each triangular flap of breast and dabbed at the pinkish shine beneath.

But the thin ones still have it better though, she thought. The fat ones weren't so shrivelled but their skins rubbed, the folds were damp and hot. She thought of her first morning, doing a shift with Mr Peters himself, and him demonstrating:

'. . . And the skin here can get very hot and damp, d'you see? And that means' (dropping his voice) 'it *grows* things.'

Binnie had had to turn aside from blank immobile Mrs Bellingham, whose tiered and frilly abdomen was possibly growing several varieties of thing, and take a few deep breaths.

'But then I thought, Hold on!' cried Mrs Simmonds, suddenly opening her eyes as Binnie drew the clean vest down over her head, 'hold on, Top of the morning to you, no, he was that film star – '

By stretching the vest's armholes to their fullest extent

Binnie could just get Mrs Simmonds's hooked arms in, right . . . left . . .

'He was that Tyrone Power!'

'What?'

'Tyrone Power,' said Mrs Simmonds triumphantly.

'You knew Tyrone Power?'

'No no no. My dear girl. I remembered the scene. I thought he was talking to me. But he was someone from a film, talking to someone else in a film, d'you see?'

Binnie nodded. 'Ah.'

'Yes. He was someone else's memory. And I thought, do you *know* – '

She paused, for effect, but for too long, as the very old tend to, as if the sense of timing slows down along with everything else. Binnie was perfectly used to this by now, and patient.

'No, what?' she prompted finally.

'I thought, the trouble with my memory *is*, it's not so much fading away as getting better all the time, I concentrate and all sorts of memories come back so clearly *but*, most of them aren't mine at all, they're someone else's!'

'Like stray dogs.'

'Exactly!' cried Mrs Simmonds eagerly. 'You've got it, *exactly* like stray dogs rushing up when you whistle, jolly clever!'

Binnie blushed.

'Mainly from the cinema, I think, also novels and of course pictures in magazines . . .'

But how could you tell the difference, thought Binnie as she folded up the towel and poked it over the radiator. Real memories, your own, look like bits of film anyway, or photographs; you remember them from the outside even if you're in them at the same time, the way you can be in dreams.

And if the stray memories didn't have any obvious clues in them, Tyrone Power kissing his fingers to you, or that favourite blouse turning out on closer inspection to have the Queen Mother inside it, how would you ever tell the difference, when you got old?

Perhaps you just had to abandon the whole lot, the entire weight of real and stray, remembered and borrowed. The suitcase gets too heavy for you, thought Binnie.

Tell Em to put her coat on, will you?

Evidently Peter.

My birthday's in December.

'Got to be off now,' said Binnie. 'I'll be bringing your coffee in later, all right?'

'So nice to see you,' said Mrs Simmonds drowsily, 'and drive carefully now, darling, won't you.'

'Right you are,' said Binnie, and she gently closed the door.

Eight

It was nearly ten to eleven before Julia got to work; as she limped to the cloakroom she head Gerry's radio just starting on a polite morning psalm. Still, it wasn't as late as she had feared, and things in the mirror weren't too bad either, the long scratch down her left cheek obviously very superficial, the bruise on the other side more than half covered by her hair if she let it fall forwards, like this.

Gingerly she washed her scraped and gritty palms. It had all happened so fast; drawing up beside the hot breath of a double decker at a changing light she had moved off too quickly and wobbled into its great shuddering flank. She had barely touched it but it had shouldered her roughly sideways all the same, bashing her down hard onto the pavement, where she had skinned her palms, knocked her cheekbone on the handlebar, and greasily torn her tights on the chain.

The pavement was stunningly hard. Julia had lain on it for several seconds, just marvelling. She would have preferred to get up slowly, groaning, but the small crowd that had suddenly appeared all around her seemed so anxious and upset that she had felt bound to reassure everyone by being tremendously nonchalant and breezy, hobbling away as quickly as possible despite the pain and the strange metallic harp-like noises produced by the front wheel's trailing spokes.

Perhaps her wan and battered appearance would mollify even Frederick, she thought, and suddenly she snorted hard and clutched at the basin, bent with uncontrollable giggles. All that trouble climbing over the fence into the Redways' back garden, getting horribly tangled up in the thorns, strung up all over like someone in No Man's Land barbed wire, and then finding the Redways' tall back gate locked, and having no alternative but to clamber over the Redways' own wobbly thorn-beset fencing into the completely unknown territory next door. And then the worst bit: that dog skidding up baying like the Hound of the Baskervilles, jumping up and down snapping its terrible jaws while Julia simply stood still, mute with terror, not daring to move so much as her eyeballs until the beast suddenly ran off into a corner, scrabbled under a rosebush, and backed out carrying a small blue rubber teddy bear with a squeaker inside. It had dropped this at Julia's feet, and wagged its stub of tail.

Trembling Julia had slowly stooped, fumbled the bear into her fingers, straightened, and stiffly thrown it as hard as she could into the furthest flowerbed's tangled undergrowth.

How the dog had sprung after it, its horrid muscley shoulders bursting with ferocious energy! How its seamed and naked bottom had waggled as it ran! Julia herself, meeting yet another tall padlocked gate, had somehow swarmed up and over it using the handle as a toe-hold, vaulting the top like a commando in a war film.

Sorry I'm late, she imagined herself telling Frederick now. Had a bit of trouble getting here –

Still laughing so much she had to stop every now and then to lean whooping against the basin she worked her shredded tights off and lobbed them into the bin. Her naked legs were a sobering sight.

God, bruised all the way down, looks terrible, and these bloody corner-shop tights are no help, American bleeding tan, nasty orange won't cover anything . . .

Grimacing Julia worked everything into place, scrabbled fruitlessly for a hairbrush through the otherwise comprehensive contents of her handbag, pulled her hair about a little with her fingers, and set off rather glumly down the corridor.

He'll be nice as pie, she thought. Just dock me all my study time. And make me stay late all week, when I'm so tired already.

She remembered her sleeplessness, and the reason for it, and then by some mental sidestep also recalled the pot of apricot yoghurt she had stolen the night before.

Oh no! And there was a freezer-thing in the shop, I stood beside it queueing, so pleased with myself for having noticed the shop in the first place and thinking to get some new tights, oh, so efficient.

Worse she remembered nearly remembering earlier, at breakfast; felt the toasted crumpet in her hand, saw herself lightly and carelessly thinking of something else.

Bloody typical, you *idiot*, thought Julia to herself savagely. You complete fool! She would never have been so unkind to anyone else.

Now you just go to that coffee-room and you take the time to leave a note, thought Julia, nastily hectoring but at the same time almost aware by now of a certain pleasure in all this neatly contained brutality.

Right now, she ordered herself, bullying and voluptuous, go on!

Sighing Julia trailed back down the corridor and opened the coffee-room door.

'Hallo.'

Julia jumped. 'Oh, hallo.' She put her hand up to her bruised cheek, hurriedly pulled it down again.

Whoever it was smiled nicely. He was sitting at the low table, holding a mug. He had curly hair, he had a blue shirt on.

For the umpteenth time that morning Julia's heart began to beat rather fast.

'You must be Dr Fern's assistant.'

'Yes,' smiled Julia helplessly. American bloody tan! She swung her handbag off her shoulder and tried to stand behind it.

'Want a coffee?'

'Oh I can't thank you,' said Julia immediately, 'I'm terribly late already, I got knocked over – '

'Oh, I – '

(Shut up, shut up about it, thought Julia desperately, but still it came out anyway)

' – by a double-decker bus – '

'Oh!' and of course he grinned, uncomfortably, well who wouldn't you twerp, it's only one up from being run over by a steam roller,

'Well, more of a glancing blow really,' said Julia, Christ brilliant recovery ha ha adrenaline, 'I just dropped in to leave a note.' She sat down and looked through her handbag again.

'Pen in here somewhere.' No don't giggle, don't be flustered.

'Er, would you – ' He was leaning forward, holding out a biro.

'Oh. Thank you.' Nicest smile; not for too long. Finding an envelope and ripping out its contents (an unread bank statement, unfortunately) Julia thought for a moment and then wrote: I'm sorry I took your yoghurt, I'll replace it tomorrow, Julia Harmon, Room 514.

'There.' She held it out for him to see. 'It wasn't yours, was it?'

But he merely shook his head. And did he look embarrassed? Panicking a little Julia went to the fridge and folded her envelope into the ringed sticky gap where she'd found the yoghurt pot, crouching so as not to give him an unadulterated view of her battered legs in these awful tights; but when she straightened up he was looking at a magazine on his lap.

'Gerry's, I expect,' he said as she passed. He smiled up at her. Julia could not bear to look for long. She glanced away, down to the magazine.

'I'm always so disappointed,' he said, 'when there isn't a problems page.'

Julia smiled, pretending she was a woman who happened to be lightly chatting, and said, she thought very successfully on the whole, that really there ought to be a magazine that was all problems and nothing else, and that if there were she would buy it.

He gave a little laugh at that, oh dear perhaps politely, and then she could think of nothing else to say. At the same time she longed to get away anyway, so that she could begin on the urgent business of violent daydreaming and going-over-the-details.

'I've really got to go now,' said Julia, remembering to hold out his biro. He reached out and held the nib, and for a moment, before she let go of the other end, caught her eye over their nearly-touching fingers.

'I'm William Solway,' he said. Filmstar eyelashes!

'Julia Harmon.'

'Nice meeting you.'

'And you,' said Julia cheerily, making at last for the door. She raced down the corridor. Everything had stopped hurting. Hurriedly she replayed various parts of the scene several times over, trying to fix his face by recalling his words, but already he had turned into something she could only approach sideways: his blue shirt, the fold and hang of it, yes, there he was. The mug in his hand, yes, there, for an instant –

She flung open the door of Frederick's little laboratory, still smiling.

The blinds were both drawn. In the gloom the two red and green lights winked at her, mirrored into a jewelled infinity; Frederick himself, blinking towards her, sat entirely crouched like a very large frog on his swivelling chair, a pair of bi-coloured plastic spectacles halfway down his nose.

All this was perfectly familiar to Julia, but still she hesitated for a moment at the doorway, snuffing at the concentration of sweet hot plastic, warmed dust, and, she thought suddenly, of trapped air, air that had been deep inside Frederick himself, sucked in, used, and expelled by him, over and over again until none of it was left untainted.

He had pushed the spectacles back up his nose; his eyes had disappeared behind one red, one green lens. He spoke, his thinnest voice.

'Aren't you coming in?'

Julia took a deep breath of her own in with her, and held it as long as she could while she gently closed the door behind her.

Nine

On the Friday night the house felt so empty, so alarmingly like a cluttered version of the empty lime-green mock-up in the lab that after a few moments' consideration William stumped noisily up the stairs to his bedroom, squeezed as much dirty washing into his holdall as possible, and back in the kitchen wrote a quick note to Lewis:

L – Back Mon, W.

Then he saw how revealing it was: something on the lines of, Well I can go away too you know, you needn't think I've been here all by myself all this time, and if I don't actually say I'm going home to Mum for the weekend you might think it's Amsterdam or somewhere, right?

It was surprising, really, how much a little note like that might say, thought William, squeezing its remnants under the flap of the choking waste-bin: a narrow escape. And anyway he'd be back himself before Lewis was. Lewis had such a talent for turning up when the lights were on and something nearly ready to eat; and then he'd sit chatting and friendly over a bottle of wine, ignoring the great wad of mail that had generally built up since his last appearance.

And it was all so effortless, worried William now, at the

same time mentally going through his holdall for his toothbrush, it's always me trying to keep up, you can't call it rivalry when he's not even trying, no I didn't pick it up, nor those trousers with the hole in the pocket –

But as he started back up the stairs he had a sudden very strong sensation of being on Stable Speed, as if somewhere else, somewhere like heaven or the stratosphere, some immense celestial version of himself had its great fingers on the keyboard, poised to jump him up the whole flight in one jokey bound.

William stood still, holding onto the bannister, trying not to think about anything except his toothbrush and the trousers with the hole in the pocket, and presently the feeling went away, leaving him damp and dizzy and doing his best with the several comforting phrases that came almost immediately to mind.

Working too hard

Need to get out more

Need a holiday

Only natural. It was only natural, come to think of it. I was just reminded of work, that's all. Obviously shouldn't have used my own home, that's all. Should've made one up.

Cautiously William began climbing again, still holding tight onto the bannister, since nothing could be held or touched in the image-house. And there: crumbs on the stair carpet. A nail sticking out. Towel over the balustrade outside the bathroom: damp.

In the bathroom he felt safer. Reality seemed more solid there, needed less tactile evidence to keep it in place. Look all right, thought William, eyeing himself in the mirror over the sink. He cupped his hands under the cold tap and splashed his face, breathing the water in a little and noisily snorting it out again. After this he felt much better, and was even able to nip back into the bedroom for the holey trousers without being too frightened by the wardrobe, which had somehow acquired a threatening suggestiveness he could not account for at all.

I really should have made one up, thought William again, sitting idle in the crowded train home. Everyone else not reading seemed to be asleep, so he closed his eyes too, to fit in. Wish I'd made one up. Nothing to it after all. Design a house; anyone could do it, anyone could have a go. William smiled, remembering childhood confusion and the housing estate brochure his father had brought home so long ago.

'Architect-designed my foot!' his mother had jeered furiously, nearly thirty years ago: moving-in day. 'Look at that! See that? Hot water pipes right through the larder, feel them, go on!'

She seemed to be feeling cheated, fobbed off with the sort of clumsy amateurish house postmen or engine-drivers might be expected to come up with. William, aged five, had half really thought this and half known it to be the sort of artless joke that in his mother's present mood might well earn him a clip round the ear, so he had kept it to himself, felt the hot water pipes when told to, shaken his head as if disgusted, and escaped into the wet rubble of the back garden as quickly as possible.

Well, Dad must've been mad, thought William now. Showing off blueprints, spreading them out on the kitchen table, taking us to see the foundations, what did he think he was doing? Look at the way she used to buy dress patterns and run the dress up all enthusiastic and then not like it on, and stick it in the back of the cupboard and never wear it. He should have known she might hate the house once she'd got it on; if she couldn't see herself in a dress from a pattern what on earth was Dad doing, expecting her to visualise a two-storey house?

Letting himself in for thirty years' grousing, that's what: about the size of the kitchen and the funny-shaped through-bloody-lounge and the shops miles and miles away and the railway far too close. Bet he'd suspected all along as well, when there was still time to pull out. Bet he felt doomed and hopeful all at once; the way she used to feel about her homemade dresses I expect.

William opened his eyes. Over the last few stops the carriage had gradually emptied. Outside distant lights fanned slowly by.

All that redecorating, and the extension and the glass-house and other tinkerings-about; what was it all for? His mother would never be satisfied. You could replace the cracked plastic sink but the kitchen would still be pokey. She'd still sniff round the half-built garage and say, 'Very nice' in that crabbed flat voice.

William sighed. If only they'd been just that little bit more middle-class, surely they would have been easier to get on with? He felt he had changed sides so often, up Mum, down Dad, vice versa. It was odd, he thought, how often he forgot what his parents' house was really like, seemed to remember some other tranquil safe retreat, with his parents in it but behaving differently, being a nice long-married Darby and Joan sort of couple welcoming their beloved wanderer home; especially at Christmas time.

Whereas in truth of course it was no refuge at all, there was always some dreary protracted wrangle going on, and he'd be angry with them for it, disappointed.

'Your dream house come true!'

William shifted uneasily in his seat. It was his own dream house that had come true, he remembered. That very evening, and all by itself. But then he noticed something, got up, crossed the empty carriage: a copy of the *Sun*, folded and tucked halfway down a seat. The *Sun*, and bought by somebody else; good-oh, thought William. He extracted it, sat down again, and with his feet up on the seat opposite turned the pages happily enough all the way home.

Ten

Sitting out in the Sunday sunshine Evie was going on about Mr Dull's childhood on the grounds that it explained many of his grosser faults, so Julia, keeping just one mental toe on the ground and thus able to say Really, Yes or Oh *no* at appropriate moments, had otherwise simply taken off, floating in fervent dreamland.

Dreamland was extremely vague in its furnishings. Generally there was a certain amount of greenery about and a big red-and-white checked cloth spread with blurrily elegant things to eat, especially French bread and strawberries. William was wearing a straw hat and braces. Barefoot, he carefully peeled Julia a pear, and held it out to her, glistening on his palm –

'You see he's never really faced it, he's just run away from it, he's always escaped commitment – '

In the three weeks since their first meeting Julia had seen the real William twice. The second time he had been leaning against the wall in the coffee-room, reading something on the noticeboard, and his shirt had happened to gape a little as he moved so that Julia, pretending to be rinsing out a mug in perfect ease, had risked a quick look sideways and caught a definite shocking glimpse of dark curly hair between the buttons.

' – but now I actually think he sees there *is* a problem, and that only he can solve it, though of course I've let him know I'll always been there for him – '

He leant now against a simple dreamland tree, breathing fast, his eyes closed, while Julia slowly undid his shirt buttons, one by one, and slid her hand inside to caress the delicious kitten-softness over his heart.

'Yikes,' murmured Julia, sliding further down in her deckchair and opening her eyes on the real world. Crumbs. Her own heart was actually pounding. Oh, and have I missed something vital?

' – so I said to him, Look, I said, after three years of it how can you expect to take me in, it's just another attempt to escape commitment – '

No.

'Yes,' said Julia aloud, nodding as if in agreement. Within she was examining dreamland and discovering without surprise its strong resemblance to a recent Mateus Rosé advert.

Lazily she looked for a moment at the whole ridiculous unstoppable business. Project yourself into various absurd scenarios: shipwrecked on desert islands with him, hiding him from the Gestapo, or merely stuck in a lift with him, and eventually these vague and exclusively B-filmish dramas would reach some sort of climax, The Kiss or (yikes) me undoing his shirt buttons and then instead of just watching I'm feeling it all as well, like being in the film as well as in the stalls.

' – and at least you've made the first real step, I said, you've faced it, that's the main thing – '

And it's only ever preliminaries, Julia realised, checking

through her collection so far. Yes; they were all just potential, nothing for adults only, nothing hard-core. Even the shirt one's waist-up. Demure daydreams, dreams I could practically show my mother! Perhaps other women go all the way and it shows in their eyes. I bet it shows in Evie's. Whereas poor old Rachel, say, she wouldn't go as far as straightening his tie, and you can see that in her eyes too, or men can.

' – but it's not going to be easy. Don't let anyone tell you it is, I told him – '

But then if I'd had more self-control in the first place, just refused to think about him at all, I'd be much better off, I wouldn't feel all dizzy just at the sight of him, I could talk to him normally, maybe actually get somewhere with him.

Though on the other hand I've never looked forward to work so much, oh, will I see him tomorrow, will I, won't I?

' – are you?'

Julia startled in her chair. 'Sorry?'

'I said, Are you all right, you were looking sort of tense or something.'

'Oh. Yes. Sorry.'

'You sure?' asked Evie coaxingly. She was in a very good mood, Julia saw; ready to be confided in. But consider what she might make of William when she was feeling less generous; it wasn't worth the risk.

'Come on,' said Evie. She smiled. 'You're laughing, what's so funny?'

'It's so ridiculous,' said Julia weakly. She made one last effort. 'No, it's nothing.'

'Oh go on, what is it?'

Julia sighed. 'Oh well – ' It was like sliding into a warm bath. 'There's this, this man – '

'Well that's obvious!'

'No, no really, I've hardly spoken to him.'

'Got to start somewhere,' said Evie stoutly.

'It's hopeless.'

'Rubbish, what's he like?'

'He's, well. He's pretty nice,' said Julia, nodding seriously. 'Doesn't know I'm there, of course.'

'What, you mean – '

'Oh we've met. Said hallo sort of thing. But he's not interested, or – '

'Ze married?'

Julia felt quite shocked. Somehow it had not occurred to her even to wonder.

'I don't know. I don't think so. He doesn't look married.'

'They never do,' said Evie darkly, as though scores of married men were lined up asking for her, thought Julia scornfully; then she remembered the one before Mr Boring, who'd apparently lasted even longer, off and on, than Mr B threatened to, and who'd kept going back to his wife the way Mr Boring kept trying to escape commitment. Perhaps it didn't matter much what it was, thought Julia uncomfortably, so long as it made for an exciting crisis now and then.

'Well you know what you've got to do, don't you,' said Evie.

'No, what?'

'Ask him out of course.'

'Oh. Oh, I can't. Oh, no.'

'Don't be useless, 'course you can. What you waiting for?'

'I can't.'

'Well, I would. Look, they love it. Men do. Honestly. They love it.'

'Chasing him.'

'No, it's being assertive. I mean, if he can't handle that, who wants him anyway?'

I do, thought Julia, rather overcome at the thought of William being unable to handle something, but aloud she said, 'It's giving away too much. You can't be all cool, can you, when you've already let them know you, well, find them attractive.'

Evie got quite heated. 'Look, you're not asking him to marry you, you're asking him out. Because he *looks* nice. You might find he's a right twit once you get talking to him.'

'I wouldn't care,' said Julia, suddenly changing tack, 'not with him looking like that.'

'You *see*,' wailed Evie, 'you'd be treating him like a sex-object, they *love* it.'

Julia laughed. 'It's no good. I can't.'

'Look. Two tickets to, I dunno, some play; Hallo, Whatshisname, what *is* his name?'

(Oh, luxury, to say his name out loud; and for the first time.)

'William.'

'Um, nice. Hallo, William, how are you, oh yes look, some friends of mine are getting up a party to go and see (you know, something nice, intellectual but sexy, right?) and I was wondering if you'd like to come along too.'

'Party? What party, I don't want to – '

'Don't be thick. It's just you and him. Oldest trick in the book. He feels safe, see, thinks there's a whole bunch of you going, sounds jolly, why not, and on the night it's just you and him. Oh yes all that fell through, you say, all innocent – '

'Evie – '

'See? That's how you do it.'

Both of them laughed. But both of us know it's not quite a joke, thought Julia.

'All this endless talking about men,' she said. 'I bet they never go on and on about us all the time.'

''Course they do,' said Evie immediately. 'Wherever two or three of them are gathered together, bars and sweaty gym clubs, they're all singing the same song, bass and tenor versions,' she waved her slender wrists about. But she doesn't really think that, Julia realised. She doesn't believe it either.

'Oh, but he is lovely,' she said aloud, shaking her head to let Evie know she didn't want to talk about it any more.

'Ah, she's in love,' crooned Evie, patting Julia's forearm, but evidently getting the message. 'D'you want some more coffee?'

'Ooh, yes please.'

Alone in the garden Julia remembered her fantasies. Was she in love because she kept daydreaming, she asked herself lightly, or daydreaming because she was in love? But it's all because I'm on my own anyway, she thought more sourly. My life's been so awful lately I have to fantasise all the time, and if it gets much worse I'll get stuck inside my dreams and go mad.

But really it was such a sunny day, the air for once so fresh and summery even in Evie's damp back garden, that it was difficult to sustain what was clearly the stern unpalatable truth for long. In fact Julia had barely got to

– stuck inside my dreams and go mad

before she and William were finding their seats in the warm darkness (seeing some intellectual but sexy play or another) and then sitting down at last to the candlelit supper somewhere cosy and intimate with red-and-white checked tablecloths and a gypsy violinist; oh do shut up, thought Julia at the lurking slack purveyor of secondhand imagery who seemed always ready to take over at the slightest opportunity, and with an effort she sat William down on the uncomfortable futon in Evie's front room and tried discussing, Oh, I don't know, Ibsen with him.

'Yes?' asked Evie, putting the coffee down.

Julia looked at her. 'No. Well,' she added, telling herself she was only saying so to keep Evie quiet, 'I'm just thinking about it, OK?'

Evie sighed theatrically and sat down.

'Of course when we first started, you know, all those years ago,'

She was off again. Mr Dull, it seemed, had done all the chasing in those days. And look where that's got Evie, thought Julia, but getting ready for take-off.

Could it, after all, be worth a try?

What have you got to lose, hissed the voice of despair.

Got a point there, Julia told it. Now shut up.

'Ready, darling?'

He held out her coat for her (dark green velvet, Evie's actually, but whose dream is this anyway?) and as he folded it about her shoulder bent a little to kiss the nape of her neck.

'Oh *no*,' said Julia aloud to Evie. Inside, to William, she turned and smiled secretively, to drive him even wilder, and spoke, rather huskily, like Lauren Bacall.

'Oh *yes*.'

Eleven

Leaning back slightly from the waist Binnie scraped furiously at the frying pan. Her face suggested someone fighting a bush fire, but Eric was used to that; it was her usual cookery expression. The furious scraping was a giveaway though. Warily he leafed through yesterday's paper. If he encouraged her to yell now, would she be all right again by the time he got home or would he merely be letting himself in for a double dose?

'There.' Binnie banged his plate down: writhing bacon, ready to shatter at the first prod, and the egg a lulu even by Binnie's cross-cookery standards, the white pocked with bubbles and edged with lacy brown, the splayed yolk set tongue-shaped. It was like a tiny horrible steam-rollered face looking up at him.

'Sorry about the yolk,' said Binnie gruffly.

'Not to worry,' said Eric, pretending to be not at all on the alert.

Binnie poured them both some tea. There was a pause. Working up to it, thought Eric, chewing with careful steadiness.

'I thought William didn't look very well,' she said at last.

Eric went on balancing bacon fragments on a piece of

white. So. It was the who-cares-most-about-our-child manoeuvre. It was the you've-just-got-no-idea ploy. Tactics. Bland denial? No: inflammatory; just what she wants. Tense concurrence? No: panic-inducing; inflammatory.

'Oh? What makes you say that?'

As usual he looked just over her left shoulder as he spoke; an unconscious habit Binnie had long since ceased to notice, though occasionally, as now, she saw it without fully registering it, and turned her temper up a notch or two as a result.

'Coming home like that.'

'What's wrong with that, nothing wrong with that.'

Binnie sighed fretfully. The real difficulty was that her main worry on her son's behalf was simply unspeakable; a reflection on herself for even coming up with it in the first place. The last thing she wanted was to face the worry squarely or discuss it, but she didn't like being alone with it either.

'He's nearly thirty-four,' said Binnie.

It was the reasonable tone in which she voiced these complete irrelevancies that Eric found so enraging. He buttered a second piece of toast rather hard.

Binnie looked out of the window, where she saw herself and Rita the day before William's sudden arrival, dragging chairs about at lunchtime, carelessly nattering.

'Oh yes, my son's doing that, you know, buying a house with a friend, sharing the mortgage.'

'Well they all do that nowadays don't they,' Rita had replied. 'I mean they just don't bother getting married any more.'

Binnie had managed to stop herself after, 'Well, actually – ' and put on a disapproving but resigned face, nodding to put Rita off any possible scenting of the truth.

Though of course I really don't know what that is, she reminded herself quickly now.

'I thought he looked a bit pale,' she said aloud.

And that first morning at the Home, doing a shift with Mr Peters; it had been clear as day what sort of men he and his partner were. I mean I've got nothing against it, thought Binnie, remembering Mr Peters and his neat pastel pullovers and tidy hair, but it's embarrassing seeing him and his partner together.

Because whenever you do you can't help but imagine them – not exactly *doing anything* with one another, but you're sort of afraid all the time that you will imagine it. So you're aware of something you'd rather not be, you're uneasy. Whereas if it was a man and a woman it'd be completely different.

If they were married. Yes. They would have to be married. Or it'd be nearly as possibly-rude as Mr Peters and his partner. And if William brought a girl home (well of course I'd be so pleased it probably wouldn't matter, but suppose he was always doing it), if he brought girls home often, there'd be that same uneasiness, because of imagining, imagining them together, it wouldn't be decent; but if he was married I could put them both in the spare room and no worries, I'd be safe somehow, no chance of nearly-thinking something wrong.

For a moment Binnie glimpsed a connection, felt the fear at the heart of virtue. But she approved the virtue too much to keep the thought going long enough to pin it down any further, and presently she noticed Eric prosing on and on about something or other, with his fingers arched together and his eyes on the distance.

And as if a switch had flicked somewhere she stopped thinking, and shifted into a sort of automatic build-up, like a small domestic Doomsday machine: he just doesn't care, all he ever thinks about is his bloody DIY, DIH I should say, he's got to D It all Himself, it's all got to be perfect, I'm not allowed to so much as pick up a paintbrush, I might as well live on my own all the company he is, always off D-ing something in the garage –

On the verge, thought Eric, noting the way her mouth was folded. Was she going to tell him what it was he was supposed to have done, or was she going to simmer away at it all day long? Either way it was all one to him, he thought, slowly draining his teacup. I am simply not involved.

'I just don't think you've got anything to worry about,' he said finally.

'Oh well you would say that,' said Binnie, abruptly getting up and crashing china about in the sink.

Once, long ago, Eric would have demanded, 'And what's that supposed to mean?' since he would have known only too well. A long fierce row would then have followed, voices low so as not to frighten the little William upstairs. It was unfortunate all round that the new houses's walls were even thinner than Eric and Binnie had imagined; a great deal of compressed venom had still made its way up the stairs to William, shivering in his dressing-gown on the top landing. Eric and Binnie still don't know about that, and William thinks he has forgotten.

'Look.' Eric, older, wiser, more alive to the subtle pleasures of non-cooperation, stood up and laid his plate down gently on the draining board. 'You've got to stop worrying about him. He's got his own life to lead.'

'What d'you mean?' cried Binnie sharply.

'Well, you know,' sid Eric, rather startled for a moment. 'He's all right. He can look after himself.'

'Oh.' She turned back to the washing up. 'You're going to be late aren't you?'

'No . . . I'm off now anyway. Bubbye then.'

'Bye.' She spoke dismissively, without turning round, exactly as if they had had the row after all. This was one of the few of her ploys that still worked, as far as Eric was concerned, and had he not been nearly late for work already he might have risen to the challenge.

But as it is I just won't give her the satisfaction, he thought instead, and he left the house without even slamming the door, though later he would be particularly short-tempered and rude to a new filing-clerk who got in his way.

Left to herself Binnie did not worry even briefly about what life was going to be like when Eric retired in a year's time, though this usually swamped her as soon as the door closed behind him. Instead she conjured up the six-year-old William, smiling, his hands behind his back, and tormented herself with him.

'Close your eyes, Mum! Look, surprise!'

A flourish: a bunch of buttercups.

'Oh lovey they *are* pretty, oh thank you . . .'

You see, you see, Binnie told herself as she scrubbed at the pan with a Brillo, that's what he was like once. What had gone wrong? If only he'd find some nice girl and get married. Only then would she feel he was safe, somehow.

He could mess about doing whatever it was he did – not photographing snakes' eyeballs any more, he'd got very shirty when she'd asked how that was going, it was something else now, playing about with binoculars or something – he could mess about as much as he liked if he'd just prove that he was all right and marry someone. As it was she could hardly bear to hear him talk about his mad incomprehensible goings-on, they were simply part of his terrible failure to grow up and behave normally and get settled down.

No family, no home of his own (that nasty sneering Lewis forsooth) no proper job, hardly any money when you came right down to it, no company car or anything; just a lot of childish mucking about and swanning off to meet hundreds of other barking-mad crackpots constantly gathering from every corner of the globe –

The front door rattled: the post. Tight-lipped Binnie went to investigate.

Hmm. A letter for me. Handwritten.

Binnie could not remember the last time anyone had written to her. It was worrying. She held the letter up to the light, inspected the illegible postmark, stared at the completely unfamiliar hand. Slightly wobbly writing, full of loops and curling capitals: an old lady's hand. Had Mrs Simmonds dashed off a note? No, of course not. Impossible. None of that lot could write at all, except perhaps Mr Pilbeam. And Mrs Bell, could she write? Would she write Evidently Peter all the time, or would it come out in words?

For God's sake, thought Binnie in exasperation, why don't you just open it? She leant the envelope up against the marmalade jar and decided to make a calming cup of coffee first. Then couldn't wait and ripped the thing open before the kettle had boiled.

Dear Bridget, she read, and flipped the single sheet over for the signature. For a moment it meant nothing at all.

Dora Fulbright?

Then she remembered.

Twelve

Another fortnight passed before Julia decided at last that she must follow Evie's advice. After all, she thought, over and over again, for two weeks is a very long time to ponder the same question during your every free waking moment, after all, I haven't much to lose.

It'll certainly be embarrassing afterwards if he won't but then I hardly ever see him anyway, and where's the shame in acting on what you want? If I don't try now I'll regret it one day, it's always best to take the risk.

It was this last thought especially that decided her. It was rather erotic in itself, made her feel lithe and even a little dangerous, someone for whom life was an adventure.

Every evening at bedtime now she would pause before the mirror, posing and inspecting. Surely, she felt, it was all rather nice, very nice in fact, far nicer than her possibly rather unpromising face might lead one to expect. But am I beautiful enough for him? Surely – Julia turned and twisted in the gentle bedside lamplight, translating what she saw: Nude with Hairbrush – surely she was.

And tonight she opened her chest of drawers and put on her latest acquisition one more time. Though very different from her usual buys it had still come from Marks and

Spencer's, which somehow made it all right, ruled out qualms both of feminism and prudery. Obviously everyone was wearing transparent lacy camisole and knicker sets if you could get them in Marks and Spencer's, they were jolly props rather than seedy accoutrements.

But would, say, William (it was still rather embarrassing to admit to herself that she had bought such things with anyone particular in mind) would, for example, William, like that sort of thing? Would he despise it, think it slavish and comical? Perhaps he would be simply old-fashioned and shocked, not realising that you could get this sort of thing in every high street these days. Would the label be enough to reassure him? Or would he, on the other hand, really go for it, and mistake what sort of girl she actually was on its account? She could hardly point to the respectable label while he was leaping upon her maddened with scornful lust.

Here Julia giggled aloud as she took the pretty things off again and folded them up.

'More goodies for my phantom sex-life,' she had said to Evie the previous Saturday afternoon, holding up the frilly knickers, and they had laughed in what seemed a perfectly uncomplicated way. Because now that she actually had someone in view (in my sights, Julia told herself, being lithe and dangerous again as she closed the underwear drawer) her night-time desperation had died down, or at least changed its character to something far less painful.

What a terrible burden all that unfocused love had been; as if, thought Julia, climbing into bed, you've always got a certain amount of love in you to be given away, and if there's no one to give it to you're stuck with it, carrying it around, a ton weight, unwieldly, gets in the way all the time. No wonder people have hopeless passions for people they've never met and never will, it's simply too uncomfortable to give all that weight of love to no one at all.

She lay back, her arms beneath her head. Even her deeper inner voices were calmer these nights. You think I'm doing something about it, don't you, thought Julia at her own excitable insides.

Well, maybe you're right. I am. I will. If I see him tomorrow I'm definitely going to say something, I'm definitely going to risk it. And for a very nasty moment she made William redden and hesitate just too long, and say what a pity, he couldn't, he was so busy these days, how about some other time perhaps, he'd have to get back to her?

'Oh no, oh God,' said Julia aloud at the thought. Though really she was almost convinced that her several weeks of concentrated longing had to have touched him somehow. Surely he couldn't be unaware, when she was constantly summoning him up with all her strength, like this?

But in the coffee-room the next morning all certainty drained away. For one thing Gerry was there as well, mysterious hairy Gerry, with his hair parted in the middle and pulled into a small dismal pony-tail like an unhappy schoolgirl's, and his sandals, and his short fat arms and legs. You'd think he'd at least wear socks, thought Julia, fervently wishing him back in his little room with whatever he was doing this year; tree-shrews? dormice? It's not natural, feet like that, you'd think at least he'd keep them covered.

For another thing actually seeing William sitting there in the flesh made her remember all too well that, though they had now met nearly six weeks earlier and chatted on several (violently exciting) occasions since, he had made no effort whatsoever to get in touch with her. He knew where she was. Why hadn't he dropped by? If he was interested at all he would have dropped by on some pretext. Wouldn't he?

But then, there was always Frederick. Everyone knew how difficult Frederick was. No doubt William was one of the many people Frederick had at some time provoked a completely unreasonable row with, so how could William then nip pleasurably by to flirt, with Frederick glowering and muttering to himself in the very same room?

'Oh hallo . . . Julia.'

(God, was that a pause? It was, it was!)

'How are you, you've met Gerry, haven't you, old Gerry?'

'Yes,' said Julia, smiling tightly, 'hallo.'

Gerry's little teeth showed briefly between his beard and his curly moustache.

'How's old Frederick these days?'

On jelly knees Julia made her way across to the steaming kettle, and trembled over the coffee jar.

'Oh, he's actually been a bit better lately, thank you.'

'Five hours a week he gives her, to do her own stuff,' William told Gerry. 'Five hours.'

'Bastard,' said Gerry agreeably. It sounded almost cosy in Australian, Julia thought.

'His last student used to cry,' said William, looking over at Julia, 'he used to wander up and down the corridor, sobbing, great big bloke he was too.'

'Oh yih?' said Gerry.

'Yih,' said William immediately. 'Mind you,' he went on in his normal voice, 'I think he was a bit funny in the first place, actually.' And both of them sniggered a little. Rather cruelly, thought Julia, and then dismissed the observation forever, though it left a certain lingering flavour behind, for her to remember when she had forgotten what provoked it.

'So . . .' said Gerry after a pause, while Julia picked out the likeliest seat and sat in it, going for careless grace with, she felt, complete success, 'Ja hear from Texas?'

'Yeah,' said William, gloomily stretching out his legs. 'They're what, six months ahead? Something like that.' Gerry shook his furry head.

'And it's money, you know. They've got the funding, they've got scope, I'm practically on my own here.'

'Oh but it's brilliant, what you've done,' said Julia warmly.

He gave her the barest smile before he went on: 'And it was a diversion in the first place, it's ways of seeing that I'm interested in, not making things to look at.' Here William spoke for a while in Visual Psychology, describing the computerised measurement of bands of light, and his attempts to connect such measurements with the perceptions of various cell-clusters within the retina; linking these perceptions to his earlier and very distinguished studies of the obligingly outsize retinal structures of the eyeballs of certain garter snakes.

'Yes, yes of course,' breathed Julia at intervals, but Gerry could only speak Neurophysiology, and so looked out of the window in silence.

'Still,' William finished at last, 'I don't know if I'm really getting anywhere. It's a distraction; just a toy, really.'

'A very grown-up toy.'

'And you can't say worse than that, can you? Actually it's more like alcohol. Nice for a bit and then you feel sick and fall over, the most I can take is twenty minutes.'

'Teething troubles,' said Julia brightly.

'Well, it's a bit more than that really – '

'But think of the potential,' Julia broke in. 'Teaching, for instance; physiology. You could mock up the human body, take everyone inside – '

'Back to the womb,' said Gerry.

'Oh easily. You could be cell-size. Or you could be a piece of toast,' she began to laugh, 'have a complete digestion-experience,' and as she spoke she seemed to feel the air lightening all around her, warming the room like sudden sunshine.

''Cept you can't take anyone with you,' said William rather excitedly, 'you're always on your own. You could all have the gear on but it'd be like watching a film on your own, separate cinemas.'

'You could hold hands!'

'You could hold hands but you'd still be on your own, I can do anything, somersaults in mid-air, I can lie on the ceiling, but only on my own, there's never going to be anyone else there.'

'Bloody frightening if there was,' said Gerry.

'That'll be sort of what happens when everyone's got one,' cried Julia, 'people'll break into one another's imagery, you know, fill your woods with bluebells, or, you have a row with someone, you come back and find they've what, had your Taj Mahal stone-cladded – '

'Put a dinosaur in your bath – '

'Put a sabre-toothed tiger in your bedroom – '

'Made a sabre-toothed anything,' said Gerry, and this completely stopped the flow; the possibility of sabre-toothed anythings, anythings-at-all, was too much for anyone to get over lightly.

'I suppose it could be a bit dangerous in a way,' said Julia eventually.

Gerry was standing up, ready to leave. William ignored him, intent on me, on me, thought Julia remembering with a jolt how desperately in love with him she was; in the excitement of talking to him as if they were simply friends she had somehow, for a moment, forgotten.

'How d'you mean?'

'See you then,' said Gerry, from the door.

'Yeah.' William told him, scarcely looking up. Julia turned round, lavishly beaming farewell.

'I don't know really,' she said at last, turning back. 'I suppose I mean, I'd feel a bit vulnerable letting anyone else in. It'd be like letting them inside your mind. Inside your visual imagination anyway.'

'I suppose that's what artists do.'

'Yes, but you're not an artist, are you,' said Julia daringly.

Yes, now he sees me, she thought in the small pause that followed. Should I speak now?

Should I?

Now?

'. . . not an artist, are you . . .'

No, thought William sadly, remembering an evening the week before. He and Gerry had nipped out quite late for a pizza, he had gone downstairs to the gents, and on the way back up he had almost missed his footing on a step that had suddenly taken on a certain livid lime-green edge, while the panicky hand he had flung out to catch at the bannister had simply gone through the diagrammatic wall beside him into what had seemed to be complete nothingness. At any rate he had felt no sensation there, no temperature, no movement of air, no humidity.

Despite the absence of positive ways in which to describe the nothingness, his hand's remembrance of it was still too vivid for him to be entirely convinced about imagining the whole thing.

Though of course, when he had blinked, he had seen at once that each concrete step really was outlined in some sort of yellowish-green paint. To make them safer, William had told himself, his trembling hand now clamped round the perfectly ordinary smooth wooden bannister. The hand looked normal too, despite its nasty experience, despite, William had thought with a dismal snicker, all that it had been through.

And later on that miserable evening he had finally got home to find that Lewis had come back, opened his mail, and gone off again. The kitchen table was littered with invitations to parties and private views, and on the back of one of them Lewis had pencilled a note:

> Hallo W, how's things? Would you take my shirts out of the machine please. Thanks, L.

The desolation of that moment brought William suddenly forwards a week. What was she saying, Whatshername, Julia?

'. . . talking of visual imagination'

Who was ? Me?

'. . . the exhibition – '

What?

'. . . You know, the Summer Exhibition,' Julia went on bravely, 'some friends and I go every year actually.'

'Oh yes,' said William politely. Had she noticed anything, had I seemed a bit mad just then? A bit out of things?

'And I thought you might like to come along, if you're free.' Two weeks' worth of planning had gone into this piece of casual spontaneity; and so much energy, so much intensity and determination and courage that when she had uttered it Julia sat back scarcely caring whether he said yes or no; the act of throwing the dice, she felt briefly, had far more significance than the way that they fell.

William meanwhile had got himself caught up remembering a particular real madman he had once seen marching down the Camden Road wearing only a pair of tattered shorts, aggressively singing and waving his arms and looking, William now saw, exactly like a great many pictures of Early Man: surly, hairy and, innocent.

Gingerly he tried the tattered shorts on to see what it felt like but was quickly baulked by a certain sad pain somewhere, along the pavement, in the air.

What had I been doing in the Camden Road anyway?

Ah. Of course. I was going to see Laura.

'William?'

William looked up, and thinking back fast caught her words and replayed them, as if they had been hanging in the air like a waiting echo since she spoke.

Sunday afternoon alone, or spent with friendly strangers, possibly boring, possibly jolly, this rather sweet little Julia among them? It was certainly a change talking to a woman who could understand his work and appreciate its importance, though of course she was hardly his type.

'Well all right then, yes, thanks a lot,' said William.

Thirteen

It was a long time since Binnie had used the Underground for anywhere other than Oxford Street, so she had a few bad moments. Changing trains at Holborn she had walked as fast as she could down the platform to the far end to read the simple route-map she remembered must be somewhere on the opposite wall, but the train had flung itself in front just before she reached it, and after a few desperate seconds of hovering she had climbed aboard with the rest, telling herself that presently she would enquire, generally, 'Oh, ah, is this right for Finsbury Park?'

But somehow once everyone was seated she had found herself unable to commit any such enormity. The doors closed, paused as if struck by thought, opened again. Should she dash out now, just in case?

Yes, quick!

But before she could do more than stiffen in her seat the doors sighed and rushed to again, and the train bore her away, juddering along for miles and miles in what was all too likely the wrong direction. Craning round to peer up at the narrow strip-map above the seats she was able to work out that Russell Square was right and Covent Garden all wrong, but found when she turned round again that she had already forgotten which was which.

This somehow happened several times, and all the while the train kept on hurtling along, giving no sign of where to, until at last it began to slow down. Binnie immediately felt much worse, panicky, as if it was Nemesis fast approaching, not a tube-stop. She got to her feet and struggled over the heaving floor to hang onto the pole by the door.

Platform, suddenly; illegibly it shot by, as if the train was going to zip straight past it without bothering to stop at all. Binnie ducked her head, turning wildly, trying to keep up with a sign long enough to read it before it flashed away.

'Where are we?' she cried aloud at last. The train shuddered to a halt, the doors opened.

'Russell Square,' said a man's voice, quiet, neutral, by Binnie's ear. Russell Square! What did that mean?

'Oh, please, is that all right for Finsbury Park?'

'Er yeah. Finsbury Park, yeah.' A different voice, behind her.

'Oh, thank you.' Embarrassed, Binnie sat down again, trying not to meet anyone's eyes. But squinting up at the map-strip was reassuring, she definitely seemed to be on the right train. Unless it branched off somewhere. If it didn't branch off somewhere, the next station ought to be King's Cross. Binnie braced herself, waiting. She counted the stops there would be if King's Cross turned up as it should. Seven; there were seven stops to go. If it was King's Cross . . . slowing down . . . it was! So now there were six stops to go. Or were there?

Binnie counted them again in terror, as if there was a strong chance of her madly getting off at the wrong stop on a miscount, as if counting might rule out reading.

At the same time she was dreadfully bothered by the

couple sitting opposite, a dingy middle-aged pair whose clothes had that warm extra-greasy rumpled look that comes from being slept in. Whenever they moved Binnie smelt strong drink; he had longish black hair, creamed backwards but swinging over his ears in several curving tails; her muddy white legs ended in scuffed high-heels.

All this would have been eye-catching enough on its own, but over her dark tatty dress the woman was wearing a grey cardigan trimmed with two large woolly pompoms hanging on strings from the collar, and as they talked and smiled, their faces close together, the man held these pompoms in his hands, squeezing and fondling them as if they were puppies, looking down at them and up again into the woman's eyes and murmuring and laughing.

Binnie thought she had never seen anything so disgusting, but at the same time she could scarcely look away; and was positively shaky with exhaustion and nerves by the time the train doors at last closed behind her on what was indubitably and cheeringly the right station. She set off down the platform, remembering that the last time she had walked along just here had been with Will more than forty years earlier; they must have arrived here dozens of times, and yet no memories of doing so arose, no matter how hard she tried to summon them. It was, she thought, as if she had a set of Will-memories, finite, like a pack of cards. She could turn them over haphazardly, or in order, but there were no more to find, not after all this time.

There were other tube train pictures, of course. They had gone out to Kew Gardens that time, the day she had first tasted wine, from the bottle he had smuggled past the wicket in a covered basket. She had bought a bag of apples. Apples and champagne.

Yes. That was me.

'You taste of apples and champagne,' he had told her. May: high grass, cow parsley.

'You taste of apples and champagne.'

A small rather dumpy elderly woman nearly walks straight past the ticket collector.

'Oi! *Oi!*'

Stops, turns, looks down to find the ticket ready concertinad in one hand.

'Sorry,' she mutters inaudibly, gives it up, and walks on.

It was a good half-hour's walk to Dora Fulbright's house. This was better, Binnie felt, than the added terror of buses, which had even more scope of getting you completely lost than tube trains. Besides the walk was full of interesting surprises, foreign shops for the foreign people thronging everywhere, women in gauzy saris and droopy acrylic cardigans, men in turbans, men with enormous bulging hats on, a boy with his hair simply standing on end. And in trays on the pavement things Binnie had never seen before were on sale with the tomatoes and the ordinary grapes; thick chunks of what looked like tree root, little shiny pointed vegetable-things like Christmas-tree decorations, bunches of wilted leaves in heaps.

Binnie looked at all these things very carefully, remarking upon them to herself, or rather, to herself but as if there were some slow-witted person inside her, who appreciated constant gentle attention and a bright running commentary, a sort of internal Mrs Bell. Enunciating clearly, Binnie put it all into slow-motion thought-words.

'Look at those extraordinary bananas, do you suppose they really are bananas when they look like that?'

'Are those yams, do you think?'

'Look at those spiky pear-things!'

'*Native* food,' explained Binnie helpfully.

The sun shone brightly, the shops breathed out their mingled gusts of spiciness and fishiness and ordinary grocery-custard smells. The pavement was studded with slender adolescent trees, 'Nice and shady one day,' their branches looped with stray cassette tape that flew out glittering in the light morning wind.

Once a young black man bent over just in front of Binnie, and set an empty Coca-Cola tin down on the pavement, carefully, as if he were balancing it there.

'How disgusting!'

Clearly no one had taught him any better. She recalled and mentally described her own child William giving her his sweetie papers to take home in her handbag: that was training.

'Should I perhaps dispose of it myself, properly?' But looking ahead she noticed how crammed to overflowing the small litter bin on the next lamp-post was; and the tin looked very nasty sitting there, somehow much nastier to the touch than a dirty cup or glass.

There is nowhere to put it anyway, thought Binnie, shepherding herself past it and over a zebra crossing. Here she had a few unpleasant moments; coming across a nice new-looking Tesco's, the actual thought of Dora Fulbright proved irrepressible.

Expect she does her shopping there then, thought Binnie without meaning to at all, and at once the awful reality of what she was doing and where she was going made her almost dizzy with anxiety. She saw herself, mute by the kitchen sink at home, one rubber glove still on, holding Dora's letter, which straight away read itself out to her again, as it had so relentlessly ever since she opened it.

My dear Bridget,
 I do hope you remember me. I remember you very well, and should like to see you again.
 I am sorry there has been no contact between us for so many years, there seemed no point, however something has happened, I have news of William and I should like you to know, you may not want to, of course, that is up to you.
 I am generally at home but if you would like to come please write to me or telephone, letting it ring properly. I look foward to seeing you,
 Yours sincerely,
 Dora Fulbright

Reaching the signature at last Binnie concentrated as fiercely as possible on the road ahead, since without such real effort the letter would go on repeating itself, first in order and then maddeningly jumbled up, in phrases: You may not want to . . . something has happened . . . generally at home . . .

Quick, what was there to remember here, think, think!

A crescent of what looked like little country cottages, thought Binnie grimly, while a passing baby in his pushchair turned his face away in fright at the glare she gave him, a crescent at the right beside a railway track. Striding along fast she reached another junction, and then stopped short beside a hardware shop full of matching saucepans and cake tins. Ahead, to the left, a wall of large engraved old murals. The dairy; I had forgotten that.

She went forwards for a better look, and at once Will had his arm round her shoulders, pointing with the other hand:

'Look, see,' he said. 'The dairymaid in that one. She's got six fingers, see?'

Strainedly Binnie stared at all the pictures in turn, found the dairymaid, and counted up again.

Yes. Still six.

Not a pack of cards, then. Not finite, even now. Or especially now.

... I have news of William ... you may not want to ...

I still don't know if I want to or not, thought Binnie dismally as she crossed the road to the pub opposite. Had this been there too when Will had counted the dairymaid's fingers? How odd the landscape of memory would be if she could really walk about in it, huge gaps everywhere and sudden looming details, whole streets missing, but not a woman's painted hand.

The pub doors were open and as she passed them she looked in at the immensity of vibrant blue carpet, and the trio of modern chirruping one-armed bandits by the door, broad-shouldered and glittering, each as tall as a man. It must be more like duelling than gambling, thought Binnie vaguely, and as she came to the crescent of remembered houses she paused in her tracks, on purpose this time, to see if she could summon Will.

But he was nowhere to be found, though they must have walked this street a dozen times; you got off the bus, Binnie remembered now, just past the dairy, you crossed over, came down this crescent and turned left across the railway bridge at the end. The cottages all looked very neat and freshly painted; the street itself seemed much narrower, which was a real puzzle until she realised that the last time she had seen it there had been no parked cars.

And there had been children playing in it, usually, hadn't there? In the evenings. A long bounding skipping rope, a chant from her own schooldays, not so distant then.

Down to Mississippi, if you miss a beat you're out!

Or am I making that up, Binnie wondered, remembering Mrs Simmonds flirting with Tyrone Power. The children could have come from the television, she thought, didn't they usually bung children out onto the streets for a bit of period atmosphere?

Well, I'm not gong to think about all that stuff any more, Binnie told herself stoutly, embarking on the last street to go. A longish hill, a few houses along at the top, and there you were. Now she was nearly there most of her earlier dread had faded.

I've had so much of my life already, what more can there be to hurt me? If it doesn't hurt my son then it can't hurt me, not really.

It was rather enjoyable thinking these grim uplifting thoughts. She made good time up the hill. At the top the houses, grand enough but surprisingly not nearly as grand as she remembered, stretched away on either side: poised, classy houses, pleased with their view.

Binnie checked her watch, her heart thudding, but calmly. A quarter to eleven. Perfect. Which one was it, now? This one? There, with the tree, the tree just the same, no bigger. Clean window, neat garden. Neatish.

Right then. If it doesn't hurt my son then it can't hurt me.

Doorbell.

Now.

Fourteen

It occurred to William on the Thursday that he would quite possibly feel a lot better if he set to and really did something about the house; not just the washing up and a quick wipe round à la Maisie but a real thorough spring-type cleaning.

He would move the furniture and clean behind things, he would defrost the fridge, he would finally get a plumber in to deal with the drip under the sink. He would get the place ready for a little repainting, perhaps. He would clean the windows.

At the thought of doing all these hard useful things William felt quite excited, and could hardly bear the hour or so he had to wait in his office before he could safely lock up and go home. Now that he had completely finished off all pending minor papers, tidied his lab as if he were vacating it and scrupulously read through every scientific journal of any interest or application at all, he had absolutely nothing left to do, except what he ought to have been doing all the time.

Ever since the episode on the pizza place steps he had been too afraid of his machinery to so much as look at it; he had taken to draping his jacket over the major screen and sitting with his back to it, staring out of the window. On

Monday evening he had stopped off at a newsagent's and bought himself a very fat paperback novel, which he was working on in concentrated bursts. William had very low expectations of novels in general, and so was not at all disappointed with this one, which was pretty hard going but certainly value for money; after three days hard at it he still had four hundred and sixty-two pages to go, and so need not think of buying another one for at least six months.

Though this last had hardly been a pleasant thought. Where would he be, in six months' time? Would he really have looked at each one of those four hundred and sixty-two pages and read every line? The pointless boredom this would entail made him almost want to cry. Surely something would happen soon, to show him what he must do?

In the meantime there was the house to work on. Perhaps moving the furniture would help, come to think of it; perhaps moving the wardrobe would somehow divest it of the sinister importance that still hung about its slanted bevelled mirror and slightly warped drawers.

He spent rather a happy half-hour in Safeway on the way home. The place was so pleasing in itself, so gleamingly clean, so crammed with pristine articles all waiting just for him. There were few others about, he could scoot down the wide, empty aisles, riding on his trolley. It felt a little like basic computer-travel, he noticed: the single straight track, the flowing lateral banks; I could've mocked-up Safeways months ago, he thought, hesitating over the various brands of floor cleaner.

Have we got any of this stuff at home?

I wish I *had* done a supermarket.

Anyway I want it all new.

A supermarket where you couldn't touch anything: very

frustrating. Or possibly like an art gallery, where touching wasn't allowed.

Harpic or Ajax?

The art gallery idea troubled him a little. He stopped scooting and wheeled his trolley round soberly like everyone else.

Rubber gloves?

He did not like to pursue the trouble, since these days such feelings tended to lead straight back to the lab and its waiting machinery.

All the same this particular uneasiness lingered like a melody, repeating itself until he recognised it and sang along with the words:

Oh no, Sunday, and art galleries with Julia! I must've been mad, thought William, panicking a little. He rounded a corner and picked up a grapefruit. But after all, he told himself, she wasn't going to be too much of a nuisance; ordinary nice-looking girls like her generally knew their place; looking back he could see that it was only the really beautiful ones who'd never take no for an answer. Nor maybe nor perhaps, for that matter. But you'd hardly need to spell anything out to a sensible fellow-scientist like Julia.

He scratched at the grapefruit and sniffed it luxuriously. The others would assume that he was hers, that was the only thing. Still. No doubt there would be ways of making his position clear, if need be. Though on the whole he doubted it; women like Julia tended to have friends just like themselves. He hoped they wouldn't at any rate be earnest art-lovers, the sort who couldn't just look at something but had to have a go at summing it up in one or two telling phrases; several uninteresting mates of Julia's all at it at once would be pretty hard to bear.

Though of course the fact is, I just hate art galleries

anyway, thought William, balancing the grapefruit on top of the Ajax tin. Even now, after all these years, he told himself enjoyably, as he set off towards the check-out. How old was I, six, seven? I got so bored, all that standing about, and I wandered off on my own, and got lost.

God, even now, that complete terror; lost in a whole city, walking faster and faster up and down those endless bloody corridors, not calling because it was an art gallery, it was too quiet to yell in; and all of them looking the same, a maze of rooms all leading me round and round, and then I thought I saw her, Mum, Mum! Right away at the end of the next room, I saw her green coat and her hair curling over the collar; but there were other people in the way, and a man bent and caught me hard by the elbow and hissed at me. Not to be so rude, holding me there while my mother disappeared. I couldn't speak or look at him. I waited until he let me go, I was so ashamed, pushing rudely at a stranger and being told off for it, and then I squeezed by and hurried, began to run, but it was too late, and she had gone.

It was thus that William had more than once recounted this mildly harrowing tale, to various clucking sympathetic girlfriends, partly because their response was usually so gratifying, partly because it was pleasurable in itself to reveal his mother's more noticeable episodes of carelessness or neglect. It felt a little like revenge, shopping her to other women.

And then when I found her (wry smile, shrug) just ran into her round a corner, she hadn't even noticed I'd been gone; no idea.

'Eleven pound twenty please.'

'Oh, right.'

Revenge: for the time she had failed to notice the tide

coming in and nearly drowned them both, panicking, still madly trying to carry the picnic basket as well while the water was lapping at his chin; for the time she'd forgotten sports day and missed his high jump record, and he'd thought she'd been there, mistaken someone else's hat for hers, and bounded up full of joy towards a stranger; for punctuating the tale of some fresh academic triumph with Any more cabbage, Eric? or Oh no, forgot the parsnips! for not seeming impressed, no matter what he did; for being so preoccupied.

William walked along slowly, swinging the carrier bags, thinking that he was thinking about his mother while Laura broke off a shard of wax from the candle and held it out to drip in the flame. She wore a little diamante star in her hair.

'You know, you talk about your mother quite a lot, don't you?'

'Well . . . everyone does, don't they, really?'

'Everyone *did*. I mean, teenagers, that's all you talk about, practically. But you're still at it, poor old Oedipus.'

'Look, I'm not in love with my mother – '

Oh, Laura, thought William painfully, quickening his stride. And your nice warm flat full of bits of material and books about acupuncture and feminism and the Alexander Technique, and the shameless telly at the foot of the bed, and *Vogue* in the bathroom: a whole world lost to me.

'Look, I'm not in love with my mother, she's in love with me!'

And Laura had said, He'd got a point there, and wasn't the tragedy just as much Jocasta's anyway; after all the whole business was her fault in the first place, listening to dreary old soothsayers, if she'd just said fiddlesticks and hung onto the baby as a proper woman should, said Laura, what could've gone wrong?

'He could still have killed his dad.'

'D'you know I thought your father was dead. For ages. You never mention him at all, d'you know that? Never.'

This was not the first time that this scene had repeated itself in William's head, nearly word-perfect. But he was still not attending to it properly. At any rate he was forgetting it even as it played, as if it were some kind of mental musak, laid on by someone else and there to be more or less ignored. Only the tone of Laura's last speech grated enough to be felt.

On the attack somehow even then, thought William, turning into his own street at last. No windows were lit at number nine, no Lewis, surprise, surprise.

She'd've finished with me anyway, even if all that had never happened. That strange new Laura, crying, screaming those terrible things at him. He let himself in, fumbled the shopping onto the floor.

Laura's flat, the smells of coffee and fresh basil, and '*Eau de Rochas*: warm grapefruit, nice isn't it!'

Don't be so wet, thought William brutally. Put the lights on. Put the radio on, get to work. Move the wardrobe. Go upstairs.

Go on.

It came to William that the staircase was somehow waiting for him, lying there looking ordinary on purpose, but poised, ready to hoist him up into the shapeless dark.

'Oh Lord,' muttered William aloud, 'oh Lord, oh dear. Oh Mum.' Then quickly but quite calmly, like a man determined not to panic despite the building being ablaze, he strode up the passage, crossed the kitchen to the telephone, firmly grasped the receiver, took a deep breath, and dialled.

Fifteen

"'Course what you've got to bear in mind,' said Evie as they crossed the road to the swimming pool, 'is that he's almost certainly got someone else anyway.'

Julia felt a pang at this, but guessed that she had been intended to, which helped. It was very odd, she thought, the way Evie had been so ready to give advice and then so evidently annoyed when it was taken, or rather, when it was taken with such apparent success.

'I mean, if he's as terrific as you say he is.' Her tone was light and careless: the gauntlet, unmistakeably.

Julia pondered. How to head her off? 'Well, I think he's terrific,' she said at last, smiling, 'but we all know I'm a desperate woman.'

There was a long pause while Evie digested this. She wants William to be awful, Julia realised. She wants him to be the sort of man you're ashamed to be seen out with. But why?

She remembered a night out with Evie a few months earlier, at a sort of winebar-disco in a basement in Soho, where she'd got talking to a nice-looking man who'd said he worked for the Arts Council. They had been shouting at one another over the tremendous pounding music for a full quarter of an hour and really getting on well, Julia had thought, when Evie had suddenly appeared at her elbow, and mysteriously, in just a few minutes, conjured the young man away.

She had cut in and turned herself so that Julia was somehow standing almost behind her, she had tossed her long reddish hair about so that Julia had had to back a little out of its range. Still not realising what was happening she had hovered round to Evie's left, and Evie immediately let her into the circle, apparently completely unconscious of ever having cut her out of it. But by this time the man was simply talking to Evie; he was clearly a man who'd met the exciting one, though he was still prepared to be polite to the duller hanger-on.

Yet Evie hadn't wanted him at all, not really. He had rung her up all the following week and she had made all sorts of excuses not to see him, though never quite coldly enough to stop him trying.

'Oh, not him again!'

Eventually she had asked Julia to tell him that she had gone to France for the summer, and Julia had resentfully complied. At the time the reason for all this seemed clear enough. Six years were six years, Julia had told herself; Evie evidently felt she had to prove something, being nearly thirty-one. I hadn't known I was actually worth competing with, Julia had concluded, so perhaps I should be pleased in a way. Anyway it's still far more fun going about with Evie than it is with Sue or Kate or Rachel.

But all this present fuss, thought Julia now as she pulled out her purse at the old-fashioned turnstile, all this fuss is pretty hard to live with; I'm nervous enough already. What is it she's so cross about? It's not as if I'm having a wonderful affair with him or something, I could see her being jealous then, but one date! And even then –

Here Julia's own internal censor blew a whistle. Large parts of Julia did not want her thinking about whether William had been taken in by the few-friends ploy or not.

And even then, even then . . . the words repeated themselves without meaning until Julia became aware of them and realised she had forgotten exactly what she was thinking about.

Immediately, as if it sensed a vacuum, the terrifying prospect of the following afternoon rushed in and made her stomach seem to turn itself over for dread. I wish I hadn't done it, thought Julia dismally as she climbed into her swimming costume. I wish I'd just thought about him. It'll be a disaster, it'll be so embarrassing.

It was a cold rainy afternoon, so the pool was fairly empty, a few children determinedly splashing about in the shallow end and a dozen or so adults swimming up and down avoiding one another. There was Evie already in, doing the sort of breast-stroke that keeps your hair dry even at the back. Julia snapped her goggles on and remembered part of her earlier thoughts: Evie fussing, Evie in a temper all day long. She dived in neatly, swam half a length underwater, and emerged into her smooth fast crawl.

Why had Evie stolen the Arts Council man? Was there perhaps – she reached the end, turned, shot off again – more to it than simple competition? Suppose Evie only fancied him because I had, suppose she had so little faith in her own judgement that men had to be okayed by someone else before she could move in!

Julia finished her third length and lay on her back in a corner for a while, her eyes closed in thought. And she has to keep dragging the whole business up all the time, can't leave it alone, as if it keeps on itching. Because she told me to ask him out, and I did, and she knows that she'd never have dared. I dared, and perhaps I really shouldn't have, but all the same it wouldn't be common sense or staying cool that would hold Evie back from daring it too, it would be fear. I've got something in me that says, It's all right to take risks, there's something in reserve if it doesn't come off. And Evie hasn't.

Poor Evie, thought Julia, shooting gaily past a batch of breast-stroking bobbers. And a year ago I thought she was so frightening, so glamorous and established and grown up. And I was nearly all wrong, as wrong as Rachel is about me; except that Evie does it on purpose. Was I especially easy to convince, or would everybody have been taken in? Are most people Evie, or are most people me?

Most people are Evie, thought Julia, turning onto her back. This is one of life's great lessons. I can choose to be honest, or to lie, but Evie cannot choose. No matter what she looks like or initially seems, she's more puzzled, more adrift, and more frightened than I am. Isn't she?

'Hallo!' Panting she drew in beside Evie at the deep end. Evie hung onto the bar, rubbing at one shoulder.

'Went right into me, bloody men.'

'Single-sex swimming pools,' said Julia brightly, 'they're the only answer.' She felt suddenly happy, and so lithe and dangerous she could hardly keep still. 'Which one was it, shall I go and pull his drawers down?'

'Yes please,' said Evie, mock-pouting.

'Oh, suppose he doesn't turn up,' said Julia: a calculated throw, a piece of self-doubt to make Evie feel better about her own.

''Course he will,' said Evie, following her immediately, and, it seemed, accepting the olive branch. For a moment.

'It's only a *date*,' she added irritably, and swam away slowly with her head sticking out. All the same she seemed to be feeling better as they made their way home.

'What you wearing?' she asked, as they reached the zebra crossing. She sounded friendly, so Julia told her.

'Oh. Really.'

Julia panicked immediately. It occurred to her that Evie's uneasy temper might well be hiding nothing more complicated than remorse, for having got Julia into this mess in the first place. Suppose Evie was simply feeling guilty?

'Men just don't like coloured tights,' said Evie firmly. 'I'm sorry but there it is.'

For a moment Julia tried to cling to that last part. I'm sorry but really means I'm not at all sorry and, she reminded herself. She recalled also that recently, extremely recently, one of life's great lessons had been revealed to her for her use and protection; but it was no good. Whatever it had been, the great lesson, she had, she realised, completely forgotten it. Which is another of life's great lessons as well, I suppose, thought Julia glumly as the lights finally changed. That you learn 'em and forget 'em, over and over again.

I'll probably forget that one too.

'Tell you what,' said Evie, 'I could lend you something if you like. We could choose, sort something out. Would you like my velvet coat?'

Sixteen

Dora answered the door very promptly. At first tremendous glance she seemed unchanged, still taller and larger than Binnie and dressed to scare in well-pressed navy, with stylish feathery hair.

'Bridget, how lovely to see you, do come in.'

Binnie slunk past her into the sudden dark of the hallway, in an instant anguish of embarrassment. Had she not sat sideways once on this woman's own sofa, insolently crossing her pretty young legs and looking bored at Dora's conversation? Had she not once idly flipped open her compact and re-done her lips while this same Dora had had to hold herself in over the tea-things?

She had; she remembered it all. She had flaunted her youthfulness, used it like a stuck-out tongue. It had been her answer to everything Dora had said or had been. And here she was now, found out; caught being helplessly elderly herself. A child would think we were sisters, thought Binnie wildly. A teenager would.

'Do go in.'

Hovering confusedly in the narrow passage Binnie realised at last that Dora was walking so slowly because she was leaning on a stick, and dragging one foot.

'Oh, I'm sorry, I – ' Binnie scuttled on ahead, anxious to help somehow, anyhow, as if she could thus make amends for her nineteen-year-old self, or at least show that she had grown up as well as grown old.

'Shall I – ' Firmly she held the drawing-room door well back, pretending that it was trying to close itself as Dora approached it.

Dora pretended it was too. 'Thank you so much.'

Apart from the television set the room was much the same. The table stood as Binnie most clearly remembered it, laden with cakes and crockery.

'I believe there is coffee,' said Dora grandly, preparing to sit herself down in the armchair by the fireplace. Binnie raced over and stood behind it, as if the chair might otherwise slide backwards as Dora felt her way into it. Dora caught on here as well.

'So kind,' she murmured, leaning back and briefly closing her eyes. She was a terrible colour, thought Binnie, taking a good hard look while she could, all yellowish and purple, and her hair's gone thin. She's what, eighty-five, eighty if she's a day? Binnie saw herself sitting beside Mrs Simmonds, cosily considering how young old people really are. Well, a child might think we were sisters, she told herself, but a teenager would see the difference. Surely.

'Would you – can I get you anything?'

Dora looked up, breathing hugely in and out, her nostrils flaring.

'Perhaps you would ah, pour us both some coffee, if you wouldn't mind.'

'Oh of course, yes, right,' said Binnie gratefully, making for the table. Her hands were shaking.

'Just a little milk with mine, please.'

'Right, right.' Binnie stirred the cup busily. 'And something to eat, there's all sorts – '

'Not at the moment, thank you. But do help yourself. Ah. Thank you so much.'

Binnie trembled herself a cup and sat down nursing it.

'You have given up sugar,' said Dora accusingly.

'Oh, well, I – '

'You used to take two. In tea. Three in coffee, I believe.'

'Did I?' Binnie giggled nervously, but Dora went on relentlessly.

'You were always eating as well, as a matter of fact. It seemed to be a point of pride with you.'

'Did it?'

'Yes,' said Dora boomingly. 'It did.' She closed her eyes again, and was silent for a long while.

Binnie went on smiling politely, as if Dora had been saying quite normal things, and sipped now and then at her coffee. It was probably a stage, she thought, a phase of saying what you were thinking instead of just quietly thinking it. Had they all passed through it, Mrs Bell, Mrs Pardoe, poor old Edith? Had they all once seemed to be eccentrically speaking their minds, rather than outright losing them?

She'd sounded so with it on the telephone as well.

Has she gone to sleep?

How can I ever have thought she looked the same? It was as if I'd got the wrong glasses on. Memory glasses, 1942 glasses. Like that time I came home on leave after six months, Mum opens the door, Aren't you tall! she cries, while I'm thinking, Look how small she is! Both surprised. And of course I'd been taller than her for years. But we hadn't properly noticed it while I was still at home; both wearing 1933 glasses.

A certain small sound alerted her. Binnie leant forward, holding her breath with horror. Yes; the shrivelled pouches beneath Dora's eyes were glittering with tears.

'Oh please,' said Binnie helplessly.

Dora bent one hand round her eyes and found the neat hard handkerchief in her jacket pocket with the other. Feebly she flicked it until, gabled with starch, it more or less opened.

'Here.' Cautiously Binnie leant further forward, holding out a Kleenex from the packet in her handbag. 'Take this, it's nicer.'

There was no response, so she got up and crouched by Dora's chair, waited a few moments more, and then gently pushed the tissue into Dora's hand.

Dora took it. She did not flinch angrily away from Binnie's touch, as Binnie realised she had half-expected. 1942 gloves as well, thought Binnie.

'Are you all right?'

'I'm so sorry,' said Dora into Binnie's nice soft tissue.

'It doesn't matter,' said Binnie, patting Dora's shoulder. The patting hand registered shock. Nothing but skin and bone, thought Binnie, however is she managing, is she getting enough to eat? Who's looking after her?

'It really has been very difficult – '

'Yes, yes.'

'I simply couldn't imagine what to do for the best.'

'Here. You drink this. There, got it?'

Gently, as if she were tending Mrs Simmonds, Binnie held out the cup. 'Just a sip. There you go. Bit more?'

'Thank you. Thank you.' Dora sat back, sniffing. Binnie sat down again. Shyly they avoided one another's eyes. There was a long pause.

Binnie waited easily enough. She felt quite calm now,

and even got up after a while and cut herself a little piece of sponge cake.

'Shall I, would you like some?'

'Ah . . . no, not at the moment, thank you.'

Dora patted at her eyes and sighed. 'You're looking very well,' she said at last. 'You haven't changed a bit.'

Binnie smiled awkwardly. 'Oh, I – '

'Still so slim.'

Pause.

'I know you . . . married again,' said Dora tentatively.

'1951, yes, Eric.'

'He's a – '

'He's in management.'

'And you ah, have a family?'

'Just the one boy. Um, look. Here he is.' Binnie took out the photograph she had kept in the back of her purse now for nearly twelve years.

'Ah.' Slowly Dora took a pair of spectacles from an embroidered case in her pocket, and arranged them carefully in place.

'Ah. Very nice-looking!'

'That was when he graduated.'

'I see.'

'From Oxford.'

'Really.' Dora looked at the photograph again.

'He's a doctor now.'

'Really!'

'Of science,' added Binnie apologetically.

'Ah.'

'He does research, he's a research scientist.'

'Dear me,' said Dora. She looked up. Their eyes met.

'I don't know where he gets it from, not me anyway, he

doesn't really look like anyone either, he's a real little cuckoo, we always used to say!'

'Well, I think it's splendid,' said Dora, holding out the photograph, 'doing research, you must be very proud.'

'Yes,' said Binnie uncomfortably. She had suddenly remembered something. Exactly as the thought clearly struck her Dora looked up and asked 'What's his name?' as if she had heard the blow.

'Um ah,' said Binnie confusedly, and for an instant considered lying about it, just saying John or Terry, what would be the harm?

'William,' she said. 'He's William too.'

'Oh, oh I see.' There was a pause. Slowly Dora put her spectacles back in their case. 'Ah, was that . . . quite wise, really?'

You see, you see, Binnie flared at herself, she's saying it instead of thinking it, you've got to watch your step, she's eighty-five –

'It was his grandfather's name. Actually.' She recalled catching Eric's eye as she had severally told her sister this, and her mother, and one or two friends. 'Eric's father's name,' she explained. No one had believed her then either, she remembered. 'He was named after his grandfather.' All giving one another little looks. I remember those little looks.

'As well,' she finished wretchedly, under Dora's own questioning gaze. 'This letter,' she said, shifting about in her chair, 'you said you had news, you know.' She nodded encouragingly.

'Ah.' Dora wiped her fragile beaky nose with the tissue. 'Of course that's not really true.'

'No, that's what I – '

Dora made a sudden gesture with one hand, asking Binnie to be quiet, while energies were gathered.

'It was about a month ago,' she said at last. Binnie's heart began to gather speed.

'Yes?'

'I had a letter. From the Red Cross. Through them, you know.' She paused again. Was it for over-prolonged effect, like Mrs Simmonds, or out of pain, wondered Binnie, swallowing.

'Red Cross?' she prompted.

'Someone had been, I don't know exactly what, clearing out an office, some hut somewhere. Out there, in Java.'

'Java?'

'Yes. They were going to demolish it. For development. Or something. And they found a lot of mail, a sack. Or a boxful, I don't know the details, but there were letters.'

'What, you mean . . .'

'From Allied prisoners of war. And to them. There all these years. In this hut place.'

'Oh,' said Binnie.

'It was a very kind letter, from the Red Cross, from someone there anyway, rather an odd name, Scandinavian I think. She said – it was a woman – she said they couldn't just throw them away, you see, the letters. They had a duty to send them on. To where they belonged, d'you see?'

None of this reminded Binnie of anything at all, so she had some difficulty making sense of it. 'Yes?' she said, blankly.

'Well there were two. From Will, from my William. There was one I'd written to him, unopened, and there were two from him, one to me and one to you. I've got them over there on the sideboard.'

Binnie nearly laughed. She wished powerfully that none

of this was happening. Presently she noticed that Dora was floating in a shifting area of black and yellow blotches. It was quite interesting to look at for a little while but soon began to make her feel rather sick. With her eyes closed she realised what was happening and leant forwards fast.

'Excuse me,' she said distinctly. And put her head down as far as it would go. Her tights rubbed her cheeks. She smelt the warm nylon of her petticoat through her dress, and a faint dry dusty smell from Dora's carpet. Very soon she felt better, straightened up, and cautiously opened her eyes.

'Are you all right?'

Binnie had no idea. 'I think so.'

'There's some brandy, I think, if you'd – '

'No, no.'

Pause.

'So I did have some news in a way. Didn't I? Are you sure you're all right?'

Binnie sighed shakily, nodding.

'It was such a shock to me too, at first,' said Dora. Binnie's collapse seemed to have enlivened her. She sounded excited, almost jaunty. 'I just didn't know what to do, I just couldn't take it in! Because I've got no one, you see, no family, no one at all unless you count Mrs Skeet two doors along, we play bridge. Though I'm afraid she really is getting terribly deaf these days. Refuses to wear her hearing aid, you see.'

She was slipping again, Binnie saw.

'Do you play bridge at all?'

'No,' said Binnie rather loudly. Dora fell silent. She looked nearly as absent now as poor old Edith, thought Binnie, as remote as Mrs Purdoe. Well, she told herself, getting letters from your own only long-dead son; it was enough to make anyone take a good long look at that suitcaseful of memories, test its grotesque weight one more time and finally jettison the lot. What had Dora looked like a month ago, and sounded like?

I bet she was all herself then, instead of just some of the time. But she's been unpacking ever since.

'I think *I* would like a brandy,' announced Dora.

Binnie struggled to her feet. 'Where?'

'Oh, there.'

Waiting behind the coffee pot. Binnie poured them both a measure, considering. Had Dora dreaded this, or looked forward to it? Wasn't there somewhere some small pleasure in it for her, revenge on Binnie who had stolen her boy? And not, of course, been good enough for him.

'All mothers are like that,' Will had said, yes, standing just out there, by the gatepost, 'they none of them think anyone's good enough.'

Me, I'd think anyone was good enough, thought Binnie grimly, so long as it was actually a girl. She knocked back her brandy, choked, and poured herself another one.

'Here.' She passed Dora's over, sat down. She opened her mouth, and words fell out of it.

'You never did like me, did you?'

Dora did not look surprised. She sipped her brandy.

'Well no. To be honest.' She smiled, and for an instant Will looked out of her old face, as if he winked. 'But then I didn't expect to and it wasn't anything personal. You were far too young for me to make an enemy of you. You were too young even to see that. You thought you had a fight on your hands; you were mistaken. I thought, forgive me, that you were perhaps looking at me as you looked at your own mother, who could, I think, be ah a little difficult.'

Binnie made a small snorting noise.

'But I had nothing against you, not really,' Dora went on. 'And Will loved you. We would have been friends. I assure you that one day, we would have been.'

There was a silence.

Binnie crooked her arm across her eyes, blotting her cheeks on her cardigan. 'I think I'll go now,' she said looking up, 'if you don't mind.'

'Ah no, of course.' Dora had a go at standing up, fell back, struggled again with her stick, finally made it. None of this quite registered with Binnie, remotely aware of it while she fumbled in her handbag for another Kleenex.

'Ah. It is over there.'

'Yes. I'll get it.'

There. Finger and thumb. New envelope: Dora's. Into her bag. There.

'I'll be in touch, then.'

Dora looked bewildered, as if her recent bout of 1942-self had completely exhausted her.

'Do come again,' she called, all hostess, as Binnie slid past her into the corridor.

'I'll call you,' said Binnie, giving her eyes one last dab.

'Yes, yes,' said Dora, hobbling up level. They looked at one another, and away again. Dora took a deep breath:

'I am sorry. I really am. Perhaps I should've – '

'No, you did right, you were right, honestly. I'll call, goodbye!'

Escape at last into the sunlight, still sunlight, it was still the same day, even the same morning. Binnie gulped air in, nearly ran down the path. She felt Dora watching her from the doorway, waiting no doubt for a turn, a smile and a wave. But Binnie could manage none of these, and walked guiltily away as fast as she could, holding her loaded bag very carefully and still against her side, as if it were a primed and ticking bomb.

Seventeen

Julia had a long Saturday night, kept vibrantly awake for a large part of it by a sudden access of X-certificate fantasies, set not in some vague dreamland but in the vivid here and now. These had repeated and refined themselves entirely, it had seemed to her at last, of their own volition. Eventually she had hit upon a diversion, and tried to picture herself and William quite finished with all that sort of thing for the moment and simply lying there fast asleep. After a few false starts, this had worked.

Crumbs, thought Julia, waking up suddenly at eight-thirty and remembering one or two of the more unexpected refinements, where on earth did that lot come from?

She climbed out of bed and went to the bathroom, where her own image, abnormally puffy-eyed, lank-haired and haggard, stared dismally back at her while she jeered.

Think you're hot stuff, eh?

A real porn queen!

Such cruelty made her feel quite ill, heavy all over, almost too heavy to do anything other than lean despairingly over the sink. Presently she slouched back to her bedroom, where she pulled on her jeans and a jumper that more properly belonged in the dirty linen basket, and wandered out to get the papers.

They looked like ideal reading for someone almost too nervous to sit still so she bought three to be on the safe side and managed to sit over them, sipping various cups of tea, until just after ten, when Evie came downstairs in her grey brocade silk dressing-gown, and talked about Mr Boring's latest display of idle snappishness, which had spoilt their evening out the night before and finally resulted in his going back to his place in the early hours.

'Honestly, didn't you hear us?'

'No,' said Julia. I was busy, she thought, and remembered what she had made William do in this very kitchen, just over there beside the vegetable rack. How can I ever face him again, she asked herself wanly, how will I ever be able to say a single sensible word to him when he is but isn't the man who can't so much as get through a piece of toast in the same room as me, so hectic are his desires!

She thought too of the day she had first met him; hadn't fate then really been trying to tell her something, signal perhaps that as personal disasters went he was roughly on a par with a hit-and-run double-decker bus?

'Oh Evie,' wailed Julia, hiding her face in her hands and half-joking, half not, 'I'm so scared!'

'Berk,' said Evie affectionately. 'Look, I'll help you get ready, shall I?'

Here Julia experienced her usual pang of unease, but was too fraught to look at its credentials properly. She thought instead of company and advice, and immediately felt much better, almost cheerful in fact; still nervy, but with anticipation rather than outright dread.

'Ooh, yes please.'

And so the morning had passed. Julia had bathed ('Here,

use some of this, it's supposed to help you relax'), washed her hair ('I think it'd look better with a sort of wave about here, don't you moddom?'), put on makeup and immediately taken it all off again in case he noticed the immense difference and deduced her passion for him from it, and allowed Evie to put some back on here and there ('Oh come on, just a tiny bit of colour – makes all the difference!'). She had dressed slowly, considered the flimsy underwear and rejected it not only on grounds of morality and sexual politics but also so as not to tempt fate about the future, or risk feeling unutterably sheepish and embarrassed with herself when she came to take it off again all alone later.

She had tried on Evie's yellow dress, just in case. Tried it with the other shoes. Decided on the black-and-white again. Worried about earrings ('These. Go on.') Put the velvet coat on and practised walking up and down in it. Admired her ankles. Brushed her teeth. Brushed them again. Brushed her tongue. Admitted to owning one bottle of lavender water, and that a Christmas present four years old ('Look. Marie sodding Curie wore it. Everyone knows that.') and managed in passing to eat an apple and half a piece of toast.

'It's like getting you ready to go to a party,' said Evie, making them both some more coffee as zero hour approached. 'My favourite thing, getting ready.'

'Not arriving?'

'No *don't* rub your eyes, you mustn't rub your eyes with – '

'Sorry,' said Julia, getting up and checking her reflection again in the mirror over the fireplace. 'I forgot.'

'Well don't,' said Evie rather shortly. She picked up a newspaper. She yawned. 'I hope he's worth all this,' she said.

"'Course he's not,' said Julia, smiling. All the same she had a sudden picture of Evie on the telephone in half an hour's time:

'Poor old Julia had a date, my God the *contortions*!'

This at least gave Julia something different to worry about while she stood at the bus stop. She had rather a long wait. She shifted from foot to foot, brooding. Had it all been simple cosy fun for both herself and Evie, as she had assumed at the time? She found that in retrospect it had not; that the more she thought about it the less like shared cosy fun it seemed.

She remembered the pang of unease she had felt when Evie first volunteered assistance. She thought about a scene from a novel read long ago, about two pretty girls getting a plain one ready for a ball, helping her with absolute sincerity to look her very best, since however good that was she'd never rival them.

But there's more to it than that, thought Julia, climbing onto the bus at last. You've got power over someone if you lend them props. As if: it's not your date so you send along your frock, as a proxy.

And she was laughing at me, not just with me. All that dashing up with different necklaces and calling me moddom, and the way she squished that foamy stuff onto my hair. I don't understand it. She's really done her best to make me look mine. But all the same she's made a fool of me. She's made the whole business into a joke. And I practically asked her to.

'Oh . . . fifty please.'

I suppose it makes her feel better, makes her-and-Mr-Dull look more real, that's a serious affair, not poor old Julia's pathetic buffoonery.

'Oh hell!' groaned Julia to herself, softly, against the window.

And something else too. All that fussing and preparing, it says: Julia's a real no-hoper. Tart her up all morning and she still looks a fright.

For a moment, terrible, wistful, Julia imagined being as beautiful as Evie, being someone who started off beautiful and, given a little time and effort, looked absolutely spectacular. What would it feel like to be the sort of person who made a place look glamorous just by sitting in it?

Out sometimes with Evie in one of the lulls between the bouts of Mr Boring, Julia had felt her own looks flower, so that she and Evie together added up into the sort of young women that might be glimpsed sipping wine and laughing in the background of, say, a café scene in a Truffaut comedy; or even caught lounging beside the villain's swimming pool in a James Bond film.

Feeling herself to be a possible film-prop, a charming piece of background, was one of Julia's deepest luxuries. For recently, out say with Rachel or being bored with Henry, Julia had once or twice experienced a particularly dismal sensation of guilt, on behalf of all those others in the pub or winebar whose evening had been made more drab by her presence.

Thinking about this now, and fully realising it, gave Julia a sort of energy, as if she had stretched something too far and could only bounce back.

I mean that's an absolutely *mad* way to carry on, you've got no business being so sorry for yourself. She addressed herself briskly but kindly, as someone who needed a little bucking up.

It's only a bad patch after all –

'Move along there please, move right along.'

Presently Julia fought her way off the bus through the throng of summer tourists, and as she reached the pavement remembered where she was going and with whom, and all thoughts of depression, and of Evie's possible machinations, ceased to trouble her.

(Though her sense of being subtly wronged, wronged in ways too delicate to put into words and claim redress for, will distort many future disagreements over the washing up or the puddles on the bathroom floor; Julia will not hear the coldness in her own voice as she complains again; she will tell herself that Evie has grown very touchy these days. But this is all months away.)

If he's not there I'm only giving him fifteen minutes, thought Julia, walking along fast.

No. I'll give him half an hour. Then I'm off. That'll be it.

Oh please be there, be there!

She turns the corner, crosses the busy courtyard.

Is that? Face in the paperback?

Yes!

Julia smiles casually, pushes her hair back with one hand, an unconscious but graceful gesture: one of Evie's, as it happened.

'Well hi,' she says lightly. 'Am I late?'

Eighteen

On the Sunday evening when he got home William went straight down to the basement, picked up the torch he kept there, hesitated for a moment over the stepladders but decided against them on grounds of practicality and went up and out again into the deepening twilight.

He did not think about what he was going to do, or even consider trying to telephone first, just got himself onto his bicycle and pedalled away as fast as he could along that familiar pathway, Highbury, Holloway, and freewheel it down to Camden.

Nor did he consider what he was going to say to her; dimly he recognised the need to sound completely unrehearsed. There was, he felt, nothing he was not prepared to say. If she stuck out for marriage he would somehow get over his blank nausea at the mere idea of it and say Yes of course. And Children, terrific. And, of course, Give up academic work you bet. He'd volunteer that one anyway.

Anything, Laura. Anything you want.

Her flat was in darkness. He rang the bell anyway and waited. After a while he sat down on the concrete steps before the front door.

Time passed. William got rather cold. He played with

the torch, switching it on and off again in his pocket or shining it through his fingers to make them glow red. Sometimes he got up and patrolled the pavement, stamping and swinging his arms, and generally as he did so the small remaining part of his old self, which would never have dreamt of thus wretchedly camping out on some girl's doorstep, roused itself and asked him what the hell he thought he was doing, breaking all the rules like this, betraying himself, letting her know exactly how miserable and lonely he had been without her; hadn't it been a major, even the number one comfort, imagining her imagining him having a high old time of it all these months, with dozens of other women?

Pacing again he remembered the last time he had spoken to her. 'I just rang to find out how you're doing,' she'd said, about a week after their final parting. It must have been the day before her flight, he had realised since. And (here William groaned aloud and sat down hunched upon the steps again) he had said Fine, fine, and talked about a film he'd seen the night before, using the first person plural but not too insistently, just once or twice; he had asked her how she was, without leaning on the words in any significant way, and told her to look after herself without even enquiring where in America she was going to or even (curses) how long for.

How often, since, he had relived that phone call, altering every word but her opening line! It had been such bad luck, William told himself now. I'd been feeling so angry with her. Why had she called just then? Half an hour later or earlier and it might all have been different.

Or perhaps not. Perhaps it had been too late even then, and her call had been exactly what she said it had been, a friendly enquiry and no more. He had assumed they were still playing some sort of game, the familiar power-struggle game, but I've just been playing it on my own all this time, thought William, making one hand into a fist and pressing it hard against his mouth.

Or had there been no game at all? Perhaps not. Not after all that had happened. He could see her now, lying face down on the carpet, crying into it, Laura who'd been so stylish and established and grown-up; or had she been pretending all that time? I shouldn't have said all those things, but I was so frightened, her carrying on like that.

Abruptly William stood up again and examined his watch by torchlight. Nearly ten. I've been here nearly two-and-a-half hours, he could now tell Laura, when she finally arrived. That would count for something, wouldn't it? Surely it would help.

Was it time to check now, he asked himself, or shall I wait a bit longer? Wait a bit longer, he decided. Put it off. He paced the pavement again and, as the thought formulated, simply stepped onto the low garden wall, gripped the rusty iron spears that topped it and painfully swung himself over into the dark crunchy shrubbery on the other side.

It was a place, he realised immediately, that many cats had found useful. Brick piles and potholes lurked beneath the nettles, and as he struggled over them, things with thorns, invisible in the darkness, caught at his jacket and poked through his trousers. It looked so wild and pretty too from three floors up, he remembered grimly. Sweating he fought his way through this unexpected palisade until he stood at last on the battered piece of turf the ground-floor-flat man sometimes disported himself upon on warm summer Sunday afternoons.

Now for it, he thought. Here goes.

Holding his breath William played torchlight up at Laura's kitchen window.

There. There! He bounced up and down on his toes with relief and excitement. In the torch's beam he had just been able to make out a dim greenish haze through the glass: her windowbox of herbs, the one he had carried out to her car for her before the America trip, so that she could take it to a friend. He had balanced it on the edge of the boot while she'd pushed a bag or two about, making room, and he'd said, so casually, that if she got homesick she could write to him, and she'd been very brisk in reply, not looking at him.

'I'm sorry but I never write letters.'

He could almost feel the herb box now, its splintery edges and dampish base.

Well, she'd got it back anyway. She was back. That was one fear out of the way then. But if she was back, where was she now? Sighing, William fought his way back to the railings. What was she doing, out all hours?

And he'd never once caught her on the phone. Somehow once he'd started calling, that night he'd come home with the cleaning gear, he'd been completely unable to stop, had gone on calling at three- to five-minute intervals until well past midnight, when he'd decided she must be staying with friends for the night. After two more evenings of intermittent dialling he had concluded that she was away for the week and told himself it wasn't worth trying again until after the weekend; but had rung up several times anyway to be on the safe side and because there was a definite melancholy pleasure just in dialling her number and picturing her empty flat with the telephone ringing, ringing inside it.

He could visit every room, through that ringing; call in

at each in turn as if he was on Stable Speed. He could see the faded silk cushions and the bed and the jokey little bamboo cocktail cabinet and the photograph of her mother in a silver frame; all these things sitting there silent, as if listening to the telephone he was causing to sound.

Laura, it's me, it's me!

Back on the pavement he brushed the rust from his stinging palms, and bent to unchain his bicycle. A lot of this is all Julia's fault, he told himself, straightening up and sucking on one particularly painful finger. He'd seen months earlier, almost straight away, that it was no use trying to go out with other women. A few weeks of hopefully asking out practically every nice-looking woman he knew, of going to discos and winebars and picking them up, of smiling at strangers in pubs and manipulating them into conversation on trains had showed him all too clearly that all other women, for the moment at least, were all wrong. They'd all been, somehow, so boring; so not-Laura; so wrong.

This had never happened to him before. But then it was always me that ended things before, he had told himself. Usually by going off with someone else anyway. So this was bound to be a little different; I need to wait a few months, he had decided. After all it had all been so upsetting, anyone would have been upset. I just need to wait, I was rushing things.

And now all those months of painful but necessary loneliness had been wasted! For a wild angry moment it seemed to William that he could well have been on the verge of complete recovery, that given just a week or so more on his own, he might at last have been set free. But he had weakened, pictured himself being admired and flirted with by Julia and all her little friends; had been tempted, had fallen, and now look!

Stiff with this sudden gust of anger William swung himself awkwardly into the saddle, and moved away. A couple walked by him, entwined, and vanished into the darkness.

William sighed. No; all that wouldn't do at all. Look at all those phonecalls for one thing. It was no use blaming Julia. All she'd done was show him that nothing had changed, except for the worse.

I wish her friends had turned up though. It would've been a bit better, a crowd, felt less like another endless date with the wrong woman.

And he thought: Suppose this feeling never goes away, and from now on, for the rest of my life, they are all the wrong woman, all of them, because I once knew the right one and she's left me for ever and ever amen.

Shivering William hurriedly dismounted and stood for a little while in the darkness just before the Chalk Farm Road, hoping he looked like someone having a little coughing fit. Presently he was able to control himself enough to get back on the bike, and the roar and dazzle of the main road was a comfort, he found.

He could always try again, couldn't he? She had to go home some time. And her friends: Bev and Jo and Philly; couldn't he call them up, ask after her?

It wouldn't be much fun, of course. Oh it's you, they would each say, flatly. Oh hallo, voices carefully neutral.

William pedalled along grimly, constructing various uncomfortable conversations, until he remembered that he had no telephone numbers for Bev, Jo, or Philly, that he did not know where they lived, and that he had no idea what their surnames were. And apart from one or two barely remembered parties they had all met up in pubs, or theatre foyers, or cinema queues; and it had not even been the same pub more than once or twice, so there was no local, no regular he could hopefully hang about in.

And Laura worked at home, or buzzed about all over London visiting her machinists or buying fresh bolts of cloth or delivering her extravagant dresses to at least a dozen different obscure outlets, whose names and locations he had had no clear idea of before the split, let alone all these months afterwards.

William drew up at a red light, almost ready to cry again from vexation; less than three miles, that was all the distance there was between them, and yet she might as well be lost still in America, for all that he could say to her.

He set off again and as he did so remembered for no reason at all that he could think of a pub with live music somewhere, that Laura had taken him to once, where some woman had leapt out from behind a pillar and fallen on Laura screaming about not seeing her for ages and how great it was to see her again and Hallo, who was *this*?

Whoever it had been she had given him her number. He could just see her now, tossing her long reddish hair about and hanging on his arm. Whoever she was she was in his address book somewhere: a last resort.

And in the meantime, of course! Why had he not thought of it before? He could write to her.

'I'm sorry but I never write letters.'

But he could still write to her, though, couldn't he? He would bombard her with letters, when she came home at last she'd find a pile of love and yearning on the mat waiting for her.

Or – no. Better perhaps to play it a little bit cool, just to start with, see if she responded. Perhaps just a postcard to start with. He could send one tonight. Lewis had a pile of picture postcards in his desk, and would never miss just one. Of course he would have to be a bit careful choosing the picture; he seemed to remember that Lewis tended to go for naked goddesses, or Annunciations, or Madonnas clutching babies, and clearly none of those would do.

My dear Laura, thought William experimentally. Dearest Laura? Dearest Darling Laura?

He was feeling almost cheerful by the time he got home.

Nineteen

Getting off the train at home Binnie had remembered, despite everything, that she had nothing in for tea, and so had turned and walked into the High Street, quite as if it were a normal afternoon. Though for the moment food seemed to have taken on a purely theoretical aspect; she was unable to come up with any specific examples of what counted as edible. What did she and Eric usually eat?

She reached the butcher's, and paused outside. Through the glass she saw dead animals, dismembered, chopped into meaningless little pieces and, even worse, whole limbs and organs excised and on display; a trayful of tongues, overwhelmingly tongue-like, exactly like her own, just a bit bigger, that was all; lamb's little legs amputated and skinned; rib-bones, livers, breasts. On a hook right against the glass hung a dead chicken, still swinging slightly from the butcher's hand. Its eyes were closed, and from its beak a lengthening thread of pink-stained drool swung with it, a little out of time, and ending in a tear-shaped drop of blackish blood.

Binnie went onto the the fishmonger's two doors down, where at least the fish, she felt obscurely, had after all been just fish when they had lived, not creatures that might have sniffed the summery air or galloped about in new grass looking as if they were enjoying themselves. But there was a queue, and as she waited by the counter Binnie saw a pailful of mussels set upon it on a tin tray. The pail was piled high and as she neared it one half-open mussel somehow fell out and bounced onto the counter with a tiny chinking sound. For a moment it lay still upon the glass. Then it closed itself up, very slowly, like a sigh, thought Binnie; it seemed to be sighing, rocking a little as it closed.

Death everywhere, death in the high street, death in the shops, for sale. Binnie tore her gaze from the quiet dying mussel and got out into the street again fast.

Cauliflower cheese, she remembered suddenly as she stared hard into the window of the wool shop next door, He can have that and like it and then I'll say I'm ill, I'll go upstairs and be on my own for a bit.

Already it was nearly twenty minutes since she had last read the letter, and the desire to hold it once more was so strong that for a moment she considered simply getting it out of her handbag there and then in the high street; but there was a fresh breeze blowing, fresh enough, thought Binnie, to tear at the crumbling paper. She would have to wait until she got home.

Though she knew it off by heart already, sooner even than she had mastered poor old Dora's rather more recent communication; as if she had first read it not only with her eyes but with her heart as well.

> My dearest lovely Binnie, I hope you are well and not worrying about me, I am very well. I think about you all the time. Do you remember the peacock, I think about that day often, and the house, we'll live somewhere like that one day. Look after yourself and write to me, please,

you never know, it might reach me. I know everything will be all right, believe me. I love you so much. I talk to your photograph, I kiss it goodnight. Goodnight my darling, my best girl. Don't forget me, I love you, your Will X.

Crammed onto a single sheet, torn from a notebook. Binnie saw some generous boy or perhaps senior officer carefully tearing out one page each, for everyone. The words just fitted. How long had he planned them, how had he made sure there would just be room too for the kiss at the end? Faded brownish long-ago ink, fragile paper. Opened out, four tiny holes marked the passage of some little burrowing tropical worm.

Binnie dumped the cauliflower and the cheese and the just-remembered extra bottle of milk on the kitchen table and took her handbag upstairs. On the bed she read the letter again.

My dearest lovely Binnie,

Binnie thought of Mrs Simmonds, and also of that distant Saturday morning in Selfridges, trying on hats to pass the time.

A blue-grey fedora, too young for me. And I'd thought, If I met him now, at a dance or something, he just wouldn't see me, his eyes'd flick straight past me. That was when it had started to seem a bit wrong, being thirty and still dismissing any man that gave me the time of day, on account of someone who would always be twenty-two. And I saw myself, a little old lady in a lace shawl, still married to the boy in the photograph beside the bed. A Mrs Simmonds. A tidy Miss Havisham.

I hope you are well and not worrying about me, I am very well.

And I thought, it's obvious what I should do. I had this idea that if I had real children of my own I would somehow cancel out getting old enough to be Will's mother as well.

I think about you all the time.

But I never knew when you stopped, Will. The light went out and I never realised, I went on hoping right until the end. I used to lie awake hoping. Afterwards I said I'd known all the time, but I was lying, I don't know why.

And I thought about you all the time as well, for years, until that day in Selfridges, when I saw I had to do something quick, change things, so that the life I'd had with you would be all separate and contained, not just trailing off into the present, when you were already too young to have noticed me in dance halls.

Honestly I saw all that in Selfridges. But I didn't remember it properly. I've forgotten forgetting it. Until today I'd've said, Oh yes, I was getting over it by then, 1951, yes, fully recovered really . . .

Do you remember the peacock?

No, thought Binnie, I don't. She held the letter outstretched, so that no tears would fall on it. I can't remember that at all.

I think about that day often, and the house, we will live somewhere like that one day.

I'd stopped thinking you were real, thought Binnie, wiping her face with the back of her hand. I have turned you into just a few scenes, nice pictures, and stopped believing in you. Eric and my boy, and this house and the neighbours, they've been my life. You're on top of the bus in Holloway, you're what I'll be harking back to when I'm too old to make any sense. But that's all you were. I'd forgotten you were real. I thought I'd made you up, so lovely you were.

Look after yourself and write to me please, you never know it might reach me.

Here Binnie tittered, coughing on her tears. I could write but where shall I send it to, my poor boy? Post it into the past? Heaven?

I know everything will be all right, believe me.

Ah yes. What men say to women, what women tell their children. I'm glad you didn't suffer long. That's all I ever found out, that you didn't suffer long; but died early, closed up like a sigh.

I love you so much.

Honeymoon stuff, thought Binnie, trying to remember how it had felt. But she could not; she could hardly even imagine it. Though Dora's loss seemed increasingly vivid. How can I have forgotten her so, all these years? What can it have felt like, being Dora? And it was easy to translate that sharp young face backwards into his childhood. He would have been such a nice little boy, thought Binnie, simple and affectionate and ordinarily naughty. He wouldn't have danced out of range whenever you'd needed to comb his hair or wipe his face, he wouldn't have twisted away angrily, knocking the hairbrush out of your hand.

I talk to your photograph, I kiss it goodnight.

Yes, yes, but I put you away in 1951. You're in a shoebox in the attic at the moment, with that postcard you sent me from Scarborough just after we'd met, and my ration book and my autograph album with all my WAAF friends' names in it, and Lang may your lum reek and By hook or by crook I'll be last in this book. I could dig you out later. See how you've changed.

Goodnight my darling, my best girl.

That was me, apples and champagne.

Don't forget me.

No Will, I haven't, not really, not exactly. Not at all.

I love you, your Will X.

Binnie put the letter down carefully on the bedside table, lay down, and was still for some time.

She had no name for what she was feeling. It seemed to her that it must be unprecedented, that no woman before had ever had to endure love letters from the dead, letters no one could answer, so fresh from the past.

His words, his handwriting, all brought him back so vividly, not just in isolated memory-pictures but in a sort of patchy entirety, so that lying down she could precisely recall not only, not quite fully Will, but also Eric, on their honeymoon, and the embarrassment of getting used to the differences. She could nearly remember Will's particular thrilling smell; at any rate she could remember pressing her nose against his neck as she hugged him, the better to breathe him in.

Presently Binnie got up and went into the bathroom, where she sat by the toilet waiting to be sick, but nothing happened and soon the threat of it went away.

What peacock, Will? What day was that? If it was so important that you thought of it then, how can I have forgotten it? I know I'd remember it if you could just give me a clue. What house, where?

Ah, but you were writing to that girl of twenty, weren't you, the one who was frightened of your mother, the wife you'd had all those honeymoons with. No marriage, not really. That girl would have remembered. And she can't talk to me either.

Binnie splashed her face with cold water, and thought of the trumpetings Eric made every morning, breathing water in a little and noisily snorting it out again. It occurred to her, as it had occurred to her many times before, that she should never have married him, but for the first time not on her own account, but on his. She had turned Will into a series of beautiful pictures, and ceased at last to believe that he had ever been real, but at the same time he had always been with her, the mark of perfection no real husband could ever reach.

And her William, named for the real Will: the wrong man's child; the wrong child.

Dora was right, of course, thought Binnie. Everyone had been right about that. I should never have called him William. I'd seen what to do, in Selfridges, and then somehow I'd just forgotten to do it. I hadn't kept you separate at all. Calling him after you; it was a mad thing to do.

But then I was actually pretty mad at the time. Lost my suitcase, all my luggage at once. I didn't mention that, did I, Dora? I've never told anyone, anyone who's met me since. Though sometimes I suspect they all know anyway, when I'm walking up Fairfield Drive from the Close, for instance.

'It's not shyness at all, it's vanity, they've all got better things to do than stand about looking at you all day.'

That's what Eric says. But these things leak out: me mad as a hatter in the street in my nightie on a winter's morning, with a canvas holdall, knocking on all the doors, up one side and down the other.

Look, I've got all this coal, I kept saying, all this coal, won't you take some?

And no one did anything but stare at me until I reached my aunt's house on the corner, and she got me inside and put a blanket round me by the fire, and sent for the doctor, and stood in the doorway looking out for him, and heard the whimpering; by her feet. And she knelt and tore the holdall open, and there was the baby, poor little William, the wrong man's child, just in a nappy and a blanket. Blue with cold.

So she told me.

So they all told me.

Taken away in an ambulance. I was happy to go, I remember that much.

'Oh, yes please!' I cried, when the ambulance man came in and suggested we all went for a little drive. And I told my aunt that Eric was trying to poison the baby, that he had gone mad and wanted the baby to die.

Funny, that. I *saw* him putting shoe polish into the bottle. I could swear I saw him spooning it in.

So perhaps that's why I can't remember the peacock, Will. They told me my memory might be patchy. Warned Eric anyway. It must have seemed a small price to pay for getting my sanity back, a day frizzled out here and there.

But no more children, they said. We might not get you back another time.

So that was a shame, Will, wasn't it? Things might've been better all round if I'd had children that were nothing to do with you.

Though of course that's silly, isn't it. My William's nothing to do with the real Will either.

The real Will.

Binnie began to cry again, holding a towel to her eyes. If William Fulbright was the real Will, what did that make William Solway? Perhaps it's all my fault he's the way he is, thought Binnie, not for the first time but for the first time piercingly. Cold or queer or both. On his own anyway, with no one to look after him or get him proper meals, and no family, no child to make him his parents' fellow.

Was it as a punishment for giving you the wrong father

that I seem to have been the wrong mother as well? You cuckoo child. Though I did love you, William, and I do. I did my best, I think I did. You were just the wrong man's child.

And poor old Eric. You'd think he'd have noticed. Perhaps he did. Not everyone expects to be loved in the first place, not everyone feels they deserve it, I suppose.

That Dora loved her Will. He expected to be loved all right, and he was.

And for a moment, with extraordinarily detailed clarity, Binnie remembered a picture she had once seen in a gallery. She had rarely visited such places, couldn't remember now why she had been there or when, but was standing vividly before a painting entitled, she was almost sure, 'In Paradise': a grey wet London park, drab winter, early evening; and a couple walking, the man's face hidden, turned towards the young woman on his arm, whose face, tilted up into his, was alight with desperate happiness. They were in paradise all right, those two.

Yes, I stared and stared at that picture, because I understood it. I thought, no one in this whole place can understand that picture the way I can. I didn't try to buy a postcard of it or anything, I didn't know you could. I don't know who painted it or when. But it was me and Will, waiting for the bus in Holloway, or walking down the Stroud Green Road, in paradise.

Where you should be now, Will, waiting for me. If I believed in all that. I could write to you there.

I wish I could.

I wish, I wish.

Ah, Will.

Twenty

By the time he got home William had decided to go for caution, and on the back of some portrait or another, of a rather glum-looking tatty-haired blonde, wrote

> Hallo, Laura!
> How are you? I hope you enoyed your American trip. Please give me a call sometime, I'd really love to see you,
> William

It would do, he thought, for starters; no use flinging yourself at her now. You've got to start all over again, as if from the beginning. When she called he'd suggest meeting somewhere. Nothing too loaded; not Bianchi's, scene of their first real long-ago passionate date; but dinner somewhere different, somewhere lively and light-hearted. He could picture the place very clearly, Laura's eyes merry again across the red-and-white-checked tablecloth. Lewis might know where. He would leave Lewis a note asking about it. William daydreamed constantly about this note, and spent a great deal of time running happily through the final version:

> L – I'm seeing Laura again. I want to take her somewhere really nice, got any ideas? – W

It had a casual, dashed-off look, William thought. It was just right.

Got any ideas?

And he'd let her know, when she called, how glad he was to hear from her; not giving too much away, not giving everything. That would frighten her off, he told himself. He would just let her see her chance.

But Laura did not call.

At work William kept to his office in order to avoid running into Julia in the coffee room. He brought in shop-made sandwiches and tins of Coca Cola, and sellotaped a notice to his door, requesting that no one disturb him except for an emergency. He read nearly forty pages of his novel.

But still she did not call. After the interminable weekend he rang her up again, and got the engaged signal, twice; she was back again, then, and ringing all her friends, Bev, Jo, or Philly, telling them about his postcard perhaps, and being advised to play it cool. Give her another week, he told himself, and then write again. Meanwhile, cleaning having turned out more boring much faster than he had thought it would, there was decorating. By Monday evening he had carefully moved all the dining-room furniture into the front room, spread some old sheets on the floor and painted nearly one whole wall a pale minty green.

This had some unexpected benefits: the smell of new paint, so definite, so non-graphic, altered the whole house; on the Tuesday he had run upstairs to the bathroom without even considering the possibility of Acceleration; the thought had occurred to him only when he was safely on the way down again.

Perhaps if he painted his bedroom, he told himself, he might be able to sleep in it again; the front room curtains let in so much morning light, and besides the sofa wasn't quite long enough to stretch out on, no wonder he was sleeping so badly.

The week crept by. On the second Sunday afternoon the telephone rang. William let it ring for a little, so that the time when it might still be Laura was prolonged as long as he could stand the suspense, and then snatched up the receiver.

'Hallo?'

'Oh, er, William?'

It was his father. 'Dad?' Who had never called him at home before.

'Yes, um, sorry to bother you, are you, how are things with you?' His father rambled on for a while. William looked at his watch. Laura could well be calling right now, she might be dialling and dialling and thinking he was talking to some girl and decide not to try again but to go out instead and find someone new.

'I'm sorry, Dad, look, I'm really rushed right now – '

'I think it's the job, you see, I think it's upsetting her.'

'What, the tie factory?'

'You – you're as bad as bloody she is,' said his father crossly. 'She stopped that months ago, this is the new one, you know.'

'Oh. Yes, sorry. Well look, she seems okay to me.'

'You haven't seen her for a while,' said his father, going back to sounding diffident.

'Well, why don't you just ask her?'

'You know her, she wouldn't – '

'I'm sorry, really, I've just got to go,' said William desperately. He felt as furiously impatient as if he really was hard at some intricate piece of work; and at the same time dreadfully ashamed at the lie.

His father began to apologise for having disturbed him. He was so outright humble, William could hardly bear it.

'Not at all, any time, well I mean, never mind.' Finally he got his father off the line, and re-dialled. There was no reply. She'd given up, then, and gone out. Or of course had never been trying in the first place, and he'd let his old dad down for nothing. Miserably he went back to the dining room, where the minty green looked, he noticed, just that little bit too minty. It certainly made the woodwork look rather yellow. But he could always touch that up later, he told himself. Sighing he freshened his brush. It was Lewis that had really gone for the minty green, he remembered. They had chosen it together months earlier, and left the tins piled in the cellar, where he'd come across them as he put the torch back.

He circled the wall-light, frowning. Yes, he and Lewis, choosing paint that Saturday morning, months ago. Before all the trouble with Laura began.

There was no getting away from it, not once he had realised. Since all that trouble with Laura he had hardly seen Lewis at all. William counted back as he dipped and splashed. How could he have failed to spot the connection before, he wondered. In getting on for eight months he had seen Lewis, seen him to have supper or a friendly drink with, just three times. Whereas before they were always bumping into one another, going out for a quick swim or a drink or a work-out together.

There was no doubt about it, thought William, climbing onto the stepladders to reach the highest corner, he's avoiding me. He's doing it on purpose. He must've practically moved in with that Alice.

If he really wants to move in with her I'll be homeless, I can't buy him out.

William went on painting hard.

I can't work. I'll have no home, no job, and no Laura. If this was my real house I could just lie on my back to do the ceiling.

I didn't think that. No; I didn't.

William clambered down the steps again and rested his forehead for a moment against the cold steel of the top step.

Where was I? Oh yes, he's avoiding me, And I know why. And it's not fair. The times I said to him, Look, what would you do, if you were me? And all he ever says is, I just don't know, it's never happened to me, thank God. So what's the use of that? He's got no right to carry on like this. As if it was all my fault! It was up to her, wasn't it? I said to her, If you were going to feel like this about it, why weren't you more careful, it's your business all that stuff, you took care of it, you said so –

Once more he saw her, lying on the floor in her nice warm flat, face down on the carpet, crying.

'Look, Lewis. For God's sake. What would you do? If you were me? Because she sort of did it on purpose, she took risks, that's what she says, but now she's making out she only wants it if I do, and I don't, I don't want it. She never asked me beforehand. And now, you know, it's all up to me, as if it's all my fault! What would you do?'

But Lewis would only shake his head, and look grave or peevish, and say Sorry but it was William's problem not his, and not something he felt able to advise on, because it had never happened to him, thank God.

'Well thanks very much!' William shouted suddenly, snapping his head back and glaring at his half-painted wall. 'Fat lot of help you were!' Angrily he splashed some more minty green about. 'Call yourself a friend!'

Paint spattered the window frames, dribbled down onto the skirting board.

But then, thought William, loading his brush again, I don't suppose he knew beforehand how he'd feel afterwards. About me and everything. Laura hadn't. So why should Lewis?

As if I made her do it, though. She asked me what I wanted and I told her, that's all. It was her decision.

'It's your decision,' I told her. 'It's nothing to do with me.'

'It's her decision,' I told Lewis. 'It's nothing to do with me.'

And then she turns round and says I made her do it! And Lewis never said so but that's what he thinks, I bet. And he doesn't want to know me. Well, who are you getting so fucking moral with?

William found himself in the front room, staring into the mirror. He had been shouting; he had yelled his last thoughts aloud, he realised. The echo of them seemed still to beat in the air around him, and a little puddle of pale minty green was spreading into the carpet at his feet, from the paintbrush forgotten in his hand.

Go round there now, he told himself as he knelt and busily squashed his painting rag into the creamy green. Just go round there now. It's what, it's latish Sunday afternoon, she's got to be in. Sooner or later. I'll wait all night if I have to.

But there was no need. She was in. He saw that much straight away; the front curtains were open, the pink Venetian blind was rattling against the frame. He heard it, as, his hands shaking, he locked his bicycle against the railings. The handlebars were a bit sticky and strangely greenish, he almost noticed, as he straightened up and raced round the corner to the front door. He leant on the bell. Would she stick her head out of the bathroom window as she used to, to see who it was and shout hallo?

After a very long time he heard footsteps coming down the stairs inside. The door chain rattled. Laura! He wiped his palms against his trousers, pushed his hair back. His face smiled all by itself, he couldn't begin to straighten it.

'Laura!'

The door opened, two inches. The chain was on. For a wild moment William tried to make the small dark face within into Laura's, a Laura terribly changed, tanned and wizened. A woman in a sari, anxious-looking, silent. William stared down at her, speechless himself, completely at a loss.

'Hallo.' A tiny boy in shorts and a Thomas the Tank Engine T-shirt had pushed himself in front of the woman's skirts.

William stooped. 'Hallo, what are you – ' He tried again. 'You live here?'

The little boy nodded, unsmiling.

'I'm looking for the lady,' said William slowly, 'who lives up there.' He gestured up at Laura's bathroom window. 'Do you know her?'

The boy shook his head. 'Where she live?'

'There.' William pointed at the bell. His finger, he saw, was a pale minty green. He put his hand back in his jacket pocket. 'There. Three C.'

'We live there. That one. We live there.'

'Oh, but you – ' William began, but the boy interrupted him, talking fast to his mother in some entirely foreign tongue. She talked back, surprisingly loudly, they seemed to be having quite an argument, thought William, wondering what to do next; obviously he couldn't stand here all day trying to get sense out of five-year-old foreigners.

The little boy vanished, charged up the stairs and almost immediately clattered down again. The woman took the chain off.

'Here. She leave.' He held them out, a pile of letters: real handwritten ones, bills, junk mail, postcards. Among them, William saw, the glum-looking tatty-haired blonde, the only suitable postcard.

'She say, she call for them. But she never. Two weeks. She don't come. You take them?'

'Do you know where she's gone?'

The boy shook his head, addressed his mother. She shook hers too. She had not taken her eyes off William once.

'Did she leave a forwarding address?' asked William hopelessly. 'Address? Where she is now?'

'Don't know. She say she call.'

William nodded, trying to control himself. The woman was beginning to close the door.

'And you, you live here now, three C?'

'Yes. Two weeks only.'

'Ah, two weeks, right, thank you.'

The door closed.

At the end of the road, the phone box. Last chance saloon, William told himself. Inside the kiosk he turned every page of his address book, leaving one or two pale green fingerprints here and there and, as it would turn out, glueing several leaves irrevocably together.

There. This one. Or was that the one on the aeroplane back from Sarasota?

No. It was this one. He was almost sure. Right then.

Money? Money.

Right then. Dial.

Ringing. Ringing.

'Hallo? Ah. Erm. Hallo –'

Twenty-One

It was best, Binnie felt, to carry on as if nothing had happened. In a way nothing had; or it had happened a very long time ago, like a falling star. They were supposed to have fallen years and years ago, weren't they? She remembered William getting quite heated about them years before, because she hadn't believed him.

'Honest, Mum, billions of years ago!' But it had sounded so unlikely. Surely light just went out, it didn't carry on beaming through space for years on end until it caught someone's eye down on earth, did it? How could you see the star fall, its quick shooting arc and dissolution, all in an instant, if the whole episode had taken a millenium or so to cross infinity?

'It didn't take ages to happen, it took ages to get here, can't you see?'

'Yes, but now it's got here, now what?' Was it still going on falling, for worlds further on to see? Or had it stopped, now someone had seen it?

'Oh, give me strength!'

How old had he been, seven, eight? Far too young to talk to me like that, thought Binnie now, stringing green beans at the sink.

'Close your eyes, Mum, look, surprise!'

Yes, there'd been one or two bunches of buttercups, but then arrogance, standoffishness; for years. And coming home from school with too many bruises. Of course he'd make enemies, behaving the way he did, so scornful and full of himself; but the more she'd tried to curb his showing-off and bumptiousness the worse he'd become.

And 'He's a research scientist,' she had told Dora Fulbright, but Dora had been too old and vague to make the usual assumption, the one everyone else made.

'Look, I don't have anything to do with animals,' he had told her roughly, what, five years before?

'What about those snakes' eyeballs then?' demanded Binnie aloud now, as she forced another bean into the shredder. If there were snakes there'd be other things, wouldn't there? And she'd seen a picture once, in one of his journals: a cat with wires going right into its head, through its opened-up skull, and called fig. B as if it were a diagram, a graph or something ordinary like that. The cat lay looking sleepy, with its front paws curled inwards; unaware, it seemed, of the terrible incomprehensible thing that had been done to it. It had been the unawareness that had made Binnie want to shout aloud with horror.

Was that what her William had been doing, was doing, all these years? Yes. No doubt. Whereas the real Will –

There. Done it again. I mean, thought Binnie, how much have I thought of him so, all his life? Perhaps everything I did for him and to him has always been a bit wrong, too much or too little, because he's never been the right Will, the real one; so whatever he is or might have been I've made him worse: crueller and colder. Lonelier.

And there was me knocking on Dora's door all brave thinking, If it can't hurt my son then it can't hurt me, when perhaps it's me that's hurt him all this time, the letter like a shooting star, shedding light now, beamed from the past, to show me what I've done.

Here Binnie leant across and turned the radio on, trying to shut herself up, but the instant babble of voices was also unendurable and she quickly snapped it off again. There were still some beans left to string but breaking the thrifty habits of a lifetime she wrapped them back up in the newspaper they'd come in and ruthlessly squashed them into the swing bin. But keep busy, keep moving, she told herself, and going to the stair cupboard she rather roughly manhandled out the vacuum cleaner and dragged it over the living-room floor, jerking hard on its neck so that its little red body trundled into door frames and crashed against the piano.

There, that'll teach you, was vaguely in her mind as she forced the vacuum cleaner's narrow hammer head beneath the sideboard as far as it would go; and at once she remembered her own mother, grasping some uncomprehending long-ago puppy by the scruff and pushing its little nose into a puddle of its own urine, to teach it better manners.

Binnie let the vacuum cleaner drop, switched it off, and sat down. Only a few days to go now, she told herself. Just a few days and then I'll see Dora again. That's all I'm waiting for. Everything will be better then. I'll feel better when I've talked about it. I'll tell her things. I'll be her friend. We would have been friends, I assure you that one day we would have been.

She unplugged the vacuum and carried it gently back to its cupboard, and set it to rights inside. It seemed none the worse. Poor puppy, thought Binnie vaguely. Her eyes ached. If only I could sleep, she thought.

But at night for nearly a fortnight now, ever since that day, she had mostly lain hotly awake, thinking over the usual circuit: variations on Will, Dora, William, Eric, paradise, and paradise lost.

Now and then the thoughts reached a certain grim perkiness.

After all no one really gets their first choice. Not for good, not for long. Most of us marry the Eric. Look at the neighbours, the gardening club, the WI, all those husbands, just a lot of Erics really, Erics to a man; even Rita's axe-wielding maniac just laid into the woodwork, I mean I'm very glad he didn't chop Rita up as well but it was pure Eric, just bashing bits off the door frames.

At this point Binnie would giggle to herself in the darkness, all the more helplessly because of the danger of waking up her own particular Eric lying there beside her, making the bed quiver in her desperate attempts to hold the laugh inside.

None of the other circuit-thoughts was nearly so entertaining. There were varieties of William is All my Fault, there was an I Forgot Dora, there were several ways of Telling Will about Eric. Telling Will about Eric was one of the worst. It was embarrassing, having to admit to Eric. Nightly she betrayed him.

. . . And he's got these funny eyes. I never noticed until we were married somehow, but when he's talking to you he never quite looks at you. He leans his head back a bit and looks over your shoulder: that's him talking.

And I'll tell you something else. He thinks there's only ever one right way to do everything. Boiling an egg, burping the baby, making marmalade, you name it, there's only ever one right way. He won't let you get away with any other ways either, not because they're unorthodox or a short-cut or imaginative, but they're wrong. That's why he's a DIH-er, and I can't so much as pick up a paintbrush, fifteen years that back bedroom had no plaster up and he's never going to finish that garage no matter what he says, because it's all got to be perfect, done the one right way, and he's never going to get round to it, it'd take a lifetime to get it all done right.

And he's a small man, my Eric. He's got a little office, he's got a little job. I can just see him talking at his desk, all the other people there yawning and taking the mickey, because he can't really see you when he's talking. He missed a lot of promotions, and I can see why, he'd always take the small view, concentrate on the one right way, and lean back talking about it looking into the distance . . .

Only a couple of days to go, Binnie told herself, still crouched beside the stair cupboard. Then I'll see Dora, and talk to her, and all this will stop or get better or at least be different somehow.

She put a hand on the vacuum cleaner, and patted it gently, for the long-ago puppy her mother had been so unkind to.

If only I could write back!

'Poor puppy,' said Binnie softly. 'Poor dog.'

Twenty-Two

Even during the first week, with the excitement of seeing him still buoying her up, Julia had held herself out little hope. No matter how hard she had concentrated on the good bits there was still no way in which she could make them add up to success.

He'd been on time, early even: tick.

'Hallo, you look nice!' His first words: big tick, gold star.

Seemed a little irritable while they waited: cross.

But seemed happy enough to get going with just Julia after the statutory ten minutes: tick.

Politely monosyllabic for at least the next half-hour: cross.

Didn't join in when she played Buying the Best Ones: cross.

Livened up when she'd mentioned his paper on garter snakes, obviously enjoyed discussing the work with a woman who actually understood what he was talking about and *offered to show her the very snakes involved*: five big ticks and a gold star.

Never touched her

Hadn't said anything flirtatious

Gulped his tea down, rushed off

Said We must do this again sometime
Without meaning it

Huge red cross through the whole lot.

'Oh, I know he won't call,' Julia told Evie, pretending to be convinced of it, and resigned. But still she jumped whenever the telephone rang. It was true that he had not asked for her number but as Evie had pointed out he could get that at work fairly easily.

'And he did say it had been nice,' Julia would remind herself now and then.

'Has he shown you his snakes yet?' asked Evie once or twice. Julia very much regretted mentioning this coup. It might well, she realised, become a Julia-story, the sort Evie amused people with at supper parties. Though generally Evie seemed to be doing her best to be encouraging. 'You're just being paranoid,' she had said when Julia told her about the notice on his door. 'Why should it be anything to do with you. He's got to work sometime, hasn't he? He's just working hard, I expect.'

Julia stayed away from the coffee room altogether, so that he would not feel at all pursued.

'But I don't regret it,' she told Evie, 'I'm glad I gave it a try.' She did not notice saying it more than once.

'Good for you,' purred Evie, who had noticed, and whose inclination to kick her acquaintances when they were down was generally irresistible. 'I thought you were really brave. I was quite surprised actually.' She regretted saying this straight away, when she saw its effect, and wondered, in the long silence that followed, why knowing how much she would regret the cruelty beforehand had rarely so far prevented her from giving way to it later on; but that's just the way I am, I suppose, Evie told herself philosophically, and besides, Julia's really been asking for it lately; so depressing.

The weekend came, and went.

Julia began to let the telephone ring for as long as she could stand the strain, thus prolonging the time when it might still be William calling. But it never was. The second Saturday arrived. In her daydreams it had been this particular evening that William had asked her to meet him on, for dinner and romantic conversation. She had gone into this daydream in great detail, working out what she would wear and how she would feel while getting ready. Contrasting all this with reality was very hard to bear.

'D'you fancy coming along?' asked Evie that evening just before she left. 'We're only going to the pictures. He wants to see the new *Star Wars*.'

Julia wanted to see it as well, but the thought of tagging along with Evie and Dull-face was too gruesome to consider for a moment.

'No thanks. Really, I'm fine. I'm going to stay in and get some work done.'

But she did not work at all. She shuffled some papers about and underlined a word here and there in yellow felt-tip. She daydreamed, the erotic one about the night train from Nairobi to Mombasa, and was painfully unkind to herself later on when she realised what she was doing. She flipped languidly through Evie's *Cosmopolitan*. She helped herself to some of Evie's gin. She turned the television on and then off again almost immediately as two lovers groaned and kissed before her eyes.

She wandered over to the fireplace and looked at herself in the mirror over the mantelpiece.

I'm twenty-four. I look very clever. Which I am. But not that pretty. Because I ain't.

Eyes, nose, mouth: how infinitesimal the differences in each needed to be, to be beautiful! The merest fraction off here, on there, and I'd look completely different. Just a few millimetres, that's all there is between looking like me and looking like, say, Charlotte Rampling. And the rest of me's so nice, and going to waste. Sorry, thought Julia to the rest of her body. Presently she took a little more gin to bed with her and had a short hopeless cry into her pillow, speaking his name aloud and feeling despair at the sound.

Sunday began even worse, because of nostalgia about two weeks earlier, when she had had the date to look forward to. I was so happy then, thought Julia, slinking out early to the newsagent in her jeans and the same regrettable jumper. But by ten-thirty or so she felt suddenly bored with being miserable and decided to go back to the lab for the afternoon, where she caught up with a great deal of her own work and even had tea with Rachel.

'How's Radio Man?' asked Rachel, slitting open her Kit-Kat.

'Oh, Gerry,' said Julia uncomfortably. 'He's all right, rather nice actually. If you like hobbits,' she added. She felt rather jolly on the whole; her work had gone well.

'And the other one, oh, what was he now?'

'Poultry Man,' said Julia bravely.

'Have you got to meet him yet?'

'Well, yes, actually. And oh, Rachel!' Julia blew her cheeks out comically. 'He's *gorgeous*.'

'Oh. It's not William Solway, is it?'

'What, you know him?'

'No, I've heard about him. And I saw him at that Christmas thing, he *is* rather nice.'

Julia felt entirely confused. Was he not her own special heartbreaking fate, then, but merely a good-looking chap?

It was humiliating to be simply another in a huge crowd of dazzled admirers, wasn't it? Or did that make it rather splendid just to have wangled an afternoon with him? Had a date with him the other day, she imagined herself telling Rachel, just to see the poor thing's eyes bulge the way they used to.

She'd be so impressed. But she'd expect a follow-up, wouldn't she? And I'd have to fib about it, pretend it was me who hadn't wanted to see him again instead of the other way round. I'd have to do an Evie.

'So, how's your work going?' she asked instead.

The real Evie was in the bath when Julia got home; she could smell cucumber foaming essence before she'd got the door half open. Julia changed, and lay down on the uncomfortable front room futon, and slowly ate a peach.

It's really all been a nonsense, she told herself. So it will go away much quicker than the real thing. Won't it?

The telephone rang. By reflex, it seemed, her heart began to jump about wildly. She put the peach down and let the phone ring a little, for old times' sake. She knew it couldn't be William.

'Hallo?'

'Hallo. Ah. Erm. Hallo – '

Christ, thought Julia. Her heart deafened her. She stopped chewing, stopped breathing, the better to hear his real voice, his actual voice really over the telephone as she had so often imagined it. Her body was trembling all over, quite violently. Now play it cool, thought Julia at it tenderly. Don't let on. Give us both a chance.

'This is um, William Solway.'

'I know,' said Julia lightly, 'I recognised your voice.'

There was a pause.

'What?'

'I recognised your voice,' said Julia again more loudly. 'How are you?' she added.

'Er, I'm fine, thank you. How are you?'

About a million times better for hearing from you, my darling, thought Julia rapturously. 'Can't complain,' she said, smiling. There was another longish pause. He was terribly nervous, she realised. She remembered how she had felt herself, that long-ago morning in the coffee room, willing Gerry to go, and giving herself little talkings-to about courage and risk and trying to feel lithe and dangerous. Was William going through something like that, did men get themselves into such states as well? Had all her old dates, even poor discarded Henry? Surely not, she thought, and especially surely not men like William Solway, the fame of whose beauty had spread as far as the physiology department. Julia nearly laughed aloud.

'What can I do for you?' she asked him gently, helping him out.

'Oh,' said William urgently.

For it was at this point that he at last realised why the voice at the other end sounded so familiar. At first he had blankly assumed that this wretched Evie-person was actually and instantly remembering him from the noisy pub with loud music; which had been bad enough but not nearly so unbelievably dreadful as somehow finding himself connected to the last woman on earth he felt like chatting to. What was going on? Wildly he looked down at his address book. Had he somehow dialled a slightly wrong number, and by some ludicrous serendipity managed to call this Julia at home? Or had his computer-madness grown and metamorphosed, spread giant butterfly wings over everything he touched and tried?

'Ah, what's your ah number, actually, please?'

Julia told him.

'Oh,' said William.

'You've been very busy this week,' said Julia brightly.

'Yes,' said William. The pips sounded. 'Just a sec,' he shouted over them. 'Sorry. So. How are you then?'

What a state he was in, marvelled Julia, who was feeling fairly calm herself, apart from her galloping heart. She told him once more.

'Good, good. Good.' There's no way out of this, thought William desperately, what can I do, what's happening? And then he heard his own voice, bland, practised: 'So. I was wondering if you'd like to meet up. In the week, say. For, ah, tea. Wednesday, perhaps.'

'Oh, Well. Er, I think so, I think I could. What sort of time?'

'Oh, er – '

'Because of Frederick, you see – '

'Fourish?'

'I think that's all right. Yes. I'd like to.'

'My office, fourish?'

'Right, see you then.' Oh paradise! 'Goodbye.'

'Bye then, oh, ah – '

'Yes?'

'Do you happen to know someone called, let me see, Evie, I don't know her surname, but – '

'Evie Turner? Evie Turner lives here, it's her house, I just rent a room.'

'Oh I *see*. I see. I ah, noticed you had the same number, you see – '

'Oh, what, d'you know Evie?'

'No no no, friend of a friend. You know. Though actually I'd quite like to – is she in at all?'

'What, Evie?'

'Yes. Is she there?'

'Well – '

'Could I – speak to her for a moment, please? She knows someone I know, you see, an old friend of mine actually, only we've completely lost touch, I wonder if – '

'I'll go and ask her,' said Julia, 'just a minute.' She put the receiver down, and saw her half-eaten peach beside it on the futon. Firmly she did not think about anything, but picked the peach up and ate it while she crossed the room, walked upstairs, and knocked on the bathroom door.

'Someone on the phone for you,' she called, and a terrible thought nearly surfaced, but she pushed it down again for the moment and knocked once more.

'Evie?'

'Who is it?'

It's William Solway, Julia thought, but some instinct answered for her instead: 'Someone asking about someone you know.'

Evie yanked the door open suddenly, and dripped rather crossly out onto the landing. 'Couldn't you have asked them to call back?'

'Sorry, I – '

Evie went into her bedroom, where she had an extension. She did not close the door. Julia stayed where she was, just outside the bathroom. It wasn't eavesdropping, she felt, unless you crept up closer and strained your ears, it was quite different if you just happened to be somewhere else and happened to overhear a few things. She held her breath, the better to happen to overhear them.

'Yeah,' she heard Evie say, still rather peevishly.

. . .

'Well, no. Not for ages actually.'

. . .

'Oh, well, sorry.'

. . .

'What, Jo Heal?'

. . .

'Yeah, just a minute, Hang on. Right, 263 1044.'

. . .

'Right. Okay?'

. . .

'Welcome, bye.'

Julia stepped lightly, but not too lightly, nothing to feel furtive or guilty about, into the steamy bathroom, and flushed the lavatory.

'All yours,' she said as she opened the door again.

'Ta. Wonder what that was all about.' Evie looked much more cheerful.

'What what was all about,' asked Julia hopefully, hovering on the threshold.

'No one you know,' said Evie, but kindly enough. 'Are you staying, or what?'

Damn damn damn, thought Julia, going downstairs. Then she remembered that he had actually asked her out again, maybe not for the romantic supper yet but still he had chosen her out of what were evidently hordes of other hopefuls. They had a date. That was the important thing, Surely. Julia looked at herself in the mirror, at her own thin face; and, rather sweetly she thought, smiled.

Twenty-Three

Binnie sat by Dora's bed, and waited.

'She's a bit up and down,' the nurse had told her, getting up to point out the right corner. 'Shall I put those in a vase for you?'

'Oh. Yes, please.'

'Are you a close relative?'

'No. Well, she's my mother-in-law.'

'Oh, really. Oh gosh, we didn't know she had any children – '

'I'm a widow.'

'Oh I see, I'm sorry. Here we are.'

Dora's thin mauve lips hung open a little.

'She might, you know, come round. She was bright as a button this morning. She's really up and down.'

'She was like that before,' muttered Binnie, remembering Dora at home, slipping in and out of senility as if it were a dress she wasn't sure suited.

'Would you like a cup of tea? No? Well, we'll just be over there if you need anything, right?'

Binnie sat down and smiled carefully at the poor old thing in the next bed, who stared back from her nest of pillows, as blank as Mrs Purvis. Binnie pretended she had something important to look for in her handbag, and eventually came across a clean tissue.

Well, I'm here at last, she thought at Dora as she wiped her nose. It was quite a relief to be sitting down for one thing, the day had been going on so long already and it was still only two o'clock. Two hours, then, since she had arrived at Dora's house in Finsbury Park and noticed the two empty crisps packets blown onto the front step, and the living-room curtains hanging half-drawn, and gone on wretchedly knocking and knocking, hoping all the time that Dora was upstairs somewhere having trouble getting down again, or out in the back garden and only just hearing her. Until the cough, the apologetic murmur behind her, the woman in carpet slippers by the gatepost, holding her cardigan tightly across her bosom beneath her folded arms:

'Um, I'm sorry, but are you looking for Mrs Fulbright?'

'Dora,' whispered Binnie now, 'wake up.'

''Course it could've been worse,' the neighbour had told her. 'If it had been a Friday she'd have been there the whole weekend as well, the home help only comes on the Tuesday.'

'Dora, please!'

It was a little sinister, the way the eye-lids rolled open, to uncover the mechanical blank regard.

'Dora?'

The bruised face smiled.

'Dora, it's me, Binnie, Bridget, hallo – '

Tiny bubbles of white had dried at the corners of Dora's mouth. Her voice was almost unchanged, a robust quavering.

'How very nice to see you. Oh – ' She moved her head against the pillow. 'I'm so sorry, was it today?'

'Oh, that doesn't matter,' said Binnie eagerly. 'How are you feeling?'

'I've broken my leg,' said Dora rather proudly. 'Coming down in the dark, you see. How's poor Flo, anyway?'

'Erm – '

'I think she's marvellous for her age, your mother. You can tell her I said so.'

Binnie went on smiling helplessly. She had hoped for so much, from seeing Dora; she had thought to swop horrors, check that she wasn't quite alone with them.

It's that I can't write back, d'you know what I mean?

I keep sort of writing back anyway, in my head, not to him then but to him now, as if he were my age somewhere, has he grown any older for you?

If he hadn't died who would I have been? As if, he had a potential life and so did I, and when he died his wife died too.

And Dora, in Binnie's hopeful dream, was going to say something like: Yes, I want to write back too. Now I am old enough to be his great-grandmother, isn't that strange? And all his babyhood and childhood, that seemed so important and took up my days, I was right to think them so, they were most of his life after all, no preamble but most of all there was.

I see the small circle of his life all complete, contained within my own larger circle, I can follow it all the way round, day-to-day, and not feel any of it was a waste or just a shame, but a lovely loving life in itself, that gave me twenty years of a certain sort of happiness. Others have had more of that, but some less, and some none at all, so why should I complain?

But me, what about me, Binnie had dreamed of interposing. It's as if I haven't looked at anything properly, felt it properly; I thought I had consigned him to the past but I was wrong; it's as if he's been standing at my shoulder all these years with his hands cupped over my eyes.

Not his fault. Of course not; mine. Because I'm not cut out to be a tragic heroine. That's the trouble. I didn't just pick up the knife, like in Romeo and Juliet. I sort of hung about, thinking things would get better. That's what I've done all my life.

And I want to write to him, to write back, and tell him so, tell him, You died and made me tragic, when I was just meant to be ordinary; and I've been uneasy ever since, confused, hanging about hoping things will get better. Three is no circle to my life, it encloses nothing treasured. And you have made me see all this now, you have pointed it out to me, and there is nothing I can do about it; Oh, why did you write to me?

'The nurses are terribly kind,' said Dora. 'Do tell Flo for me.'

And you're safe now, Dora, you're out of the storm I'm in, safe in sickness. You can put his letter back in the past where it came from.

'Yes, all right,' said Binnie. The neighbours said you were in hospital, and I thought of Mrs Bell and Mrs Purvis, I thought, What will Dora *say*? Something from his letter? Or from the last one she ever wrote, to me? What would it be?

My birthday's in December
Tell Em to put her coat on, will you?
Evidently, Peter.
I have news of William.
Something has happened.
Write to me.
Write to me.

Write to me.

'Hallo?' The nurse was bending over her. 'Are you all right?'

Binnie retrieved her handkerchief and wiped her eyes.

'Did she wake up?'

'Ah, yes. For a little while.'

'She . . . you mustn't blame yourself,' said the nurse shyly. Binnie looked up: poor little thing, she thought, seeing the hopeful, concerned young face. She smiled and nodded slightly, so as not to hurt the girl's feelings.

'Will you be coming again? She'll be here quite a long time, you know, traction and everything – '

She will never go home again, thought Binnie. If she ever leaves here she'll be Mrs Bell anyway, or Mrs Purvis. She's unpacking like mad, you can practically see her at it.

'Oh yes, I'll be back.' Sniffing Binnie gathered up her handbag and cardigan.

'Because some of our old ladies, there isn't anyone at all,' the nurse went on.

'Goodbye, Dora.' Binnie bent, and for the first time kissed Dora's cheek, dry and soft as a mushroom.

But that's the whole point of getting this old, she felt like telling the nurse. The only point as far as I can see: that by the time you're as old as Dora no one will be devastated by your loss. The younger you are the worse the damage, young Mrs Average dies and takes a dozen women with her, one or two irreplaceable mothers, someone's darling daughter, someone else's wife, some sisters, an adored first grandchild, a niece or two, and links in several circles of friends. When Mrs Bell dies she dies on her own. What's she to anyone now, or Mrs Purvis? Or Jean Shone, in a few years' time, or me? That's what it's for, this meaningless old age. That's all I can come up with anyway.

'Bubbye dear,' said Binnie to the nurse.

'Oh – yes, see you soon.'

Outside a heavy cold rain was falling. Binnie stood rather dazedly beneath the great concrete canopy over the front doors of the hospital, and as she hesitated there a taxi drew up and someone got out. Binnie waited for a moment, caught a suggestion of movement beside her, realised someone else had already made their mind up, and, filled with a sudden anger, a determination not to hang about missing a taxi just because she had hung about missing her life, shot forward, got there first, and slammed the door behind her.

'Yeah?'

Binnie had not been inside a London taxi for forty years. It felt very comfortable and nice. She thought of that entire month's housekeeping safe in her handbag.

'Victoria,' she said, and was driven away like the Queen.

The rain went on pelting down. A woman sprinted by, toeing it on high heels, with a plastic shopping bag held on her head. The pavements turned glossy, umbrellas shone. Binnie stared out of the window. There was reassurance in the wet loud traffic, as if the humdrum could rule out death. The buses especially looked so cosy, thought Binnie, even the new flat-faced ones, all lit up like mobile parties and their windows steamed up as if with the hectic talk within. Binnie sighed with nostalgia for her pure, pre-letter memories.

It was a very long ride. Occasionally Binnie looked over at the meter, but she had determined from the start not to worry about its final figure. I just don't care what it is, she told herself with a flicker of obscure excitement. London, intermittently familiar, filed slowly by.

'Zis weather,' said the driver eventually, during some particularly lengthy jam. 'S'always worse, zis weather.'

Binnie made some sound to indicate attention. Outside a group of derelicts were arguing in a doorway. It looked very crowded in there, the ones in the front might as well have been standing out in the rain, Binnie thought. She remembered the couple with the pom-poms and wondered if they were in there somewhere, squeezed in at the back perhaps, and still at it, handling one another's clothing in some new unusual way.

Yuk, thought Binnie, grinning. And look at that, some other poor soul, no room for him in the doorway probably, standing head hanging, out on the pavement and simply drenched, not even a coat on. The draggled jumper he wore looked a little like one she had knitted for her William. Binnie pitied the poor man's mother. Did she know what sort of life her boy was leading? A drug addict probably, thought Binnie as the taxi drew nearer. He's not that old either. Because of the jumper she went on looking, and as the taxi drew level and stopped again the wet young tramp looked up, straight into Binnie's face.

Presently he stepped closer, and bent towards the window. Binnie, speechless, opened it.

'Hallo, Mum,' said William.

Twenty-Four

'Get in,' said Binnie sharply.

'What are you doing here anyway?' William sat back, trying to ease his wet trousers over his knees.

'You're soaked!'

'I was walking about,' said William. 'What are you doing here?'

'I was visiting someone. In hospital. Look, I'll tell him to go to your house.'

'Nah. Victoria'll do me. I'll walk back.'

'Oh no you won't,' said Binnie. She leant forward, issuing redirections. 'There.' She felt very excited. In a taxi with William! He seemed much less of a stranger somehow, all wet and shivering a little. I'm in charge, thought Binnie. Aloud, but very gently and without looking at him she said, 'I wish you'd tell me what's wrong.'

William shrugged. 'Oh, nothing. Well.' He leant back, folding his arms and shaking his head to show her how unimportant the wrongness was. 'This woman actually. If you must know. Going to marry someone else.' He shrugged again.

'What, you mean you were engaged?'

'Nah. We'd split up actually. A few months ago. I

thought we'd get back together but, you know, she'd got someone else.' He looked out of the window, speaking distantly, as if he gave his mother such reports every day.

'Oh,' said Binnie.

'I'll get over it,' said William, and to cover the sudden shift of fear he felt as he spoke turned back to her. 'Who were you visiting, anyway, in hospital?'

'Oh, ah, well. My, ex-mother-in-law, I suppose you'd call her. You know. My first husband. His mother. Had you known her long?'

'Who? Oh, Laura. Yeah. Coupla years. I didn't know you were in touch with, Whatshername – '

'No, Dora, well we weren't actually, I hadn't seen her for years. I'm ever so sorry, William; about your friend.'

'Are you?' He looked over at her, at her eyes shining with sympathy. She had not spoken to him so warmly for years. It was rather touching, he thought, that she should be so obviously delighted at being confided in. And she probably thinks it's a bit of romance as well, he told himself more sourly. That's the sort of thing women her age go for, isn't it?

'So why'd you go and see her then, Whatshername, what, Fulbright I suppose?'

'Well, I got this letter, see.' It was only right, Binnie felt, to tell him about Dora's letter, and her journey to Finsbury Park, and what Dora had given her, when he had told her about his own sorrow; like a sort of balancing payment.

'God . . . God . . .' William muttered at intervals as she spoke. Binnie was warm with pleasure. It was years since she had genuinely impressed him, she thought. And she remembered ruthlessly squashing his tiresome childish bumptiousness; had it really been for his own good, or had she just been fed up with not being able to impress him back in any way, when he kept coming up with top marks and prizes? It was a very small part of Binnie's mind that debated this point while the rest of her paraphrased Will's letter, but all the same the guilty nag of it slightly interrupted the flow.

'And I really wanted to talk it over with her, see, because I hadn't told anyone, not your dad, anyone – '

'God . . . God . . . So. You had a letter from the past.'

Binnie nodded tremulously.

'And you couldn't write back!' For a terrible moment she thought he was making light of her, jeering, and she leant forward fast to look at him. His eyes were full of tears.

'Poor Mum!' said William. He began to cry. Binnie nearly laughed outright, from shock. At the same time she felt deliciously smooth inside. 'And you couldn't write back!' Had he really said that? Who was he then? And he'd wanted to get married, and been thrown over, and had wandered about in the rain, out of sadness! Who was he? Luxuriously she went on:

'And working in that Home, I was thinking about the past anyway, because of all these old folk forgetting some things and holding onto some things, and this letter made me remember so much, it was like time travel, it was like going there – '

William had stopped crying. He started talking rather incoherently about the work he was doing, some computer thing.

'See, I could do that street in Finsbury Park, you could visit it, like a 3-D diary, I could visit it too, anyone could, the physical past, preserved.'

'Yes?' said Binnie confusedly.

''Cept what's been happening *is*.' He sniffed miserably.

'I've been seeing bits of it at the wrong time. Sort of, superimposed.'

Vaguely Binnie remembered Mrs Simmonds flirting with Tyrone Power in someone else's memory. 'Oh dear!'

'It happens at home mostly. Or, I worry about it happening, I dream about it.'

'What, you're sort of, seeing things?'

William nodded tremulously.

'And you're all on your own!'

'This right?' They both jumped, startled by the intrusion. It was the driver: they had arrived.

'Oh, yes, sorry.' Binnie paid the enormous bill without really noticing it at all, though she decided unconsciously to keep all the change. The rain had eased off. Binnie skirted the dripping unkempt hedge. 'All right?'

William was waiting on the doorstep. Would it still happen, he wondered, when someone else is here? Go on, then, he dared his house. He felt it holding its breath, waiting for the moment when he relaxed, when it would pretend to spin on its axis like a Catherine wheel or turn its stairs into lime-green diagrammatic escalators, or seem to float upwards like a hot-air balloon. It had grown very inventive lately.

Go on then!

'All right?' Binnie hesitated beside him on the threshold. She sniffed. 'You been decorating?'

'Yes. Sorry it's such a mess.'

Binnie went into the kitchen. 'I thought you had someone in to clean?'

'I think she's on holiday or something.'

Binnie opened the fridge, looked inside, and slammed it shut again.

'You go and have a hot bath,' she said. 'I'll clear up a bit, shall I?'

'Oh, thanks,' said William automatically. 'I know there's milk,' he added, 'I got it this morning, you don't need to go out again.' He would, he thought, be able to hear her footsteps from the bathroom. He looked forward to it.

'Right then. Off you go then.' She was tying the apron on.

'Right . . . thanks . . .'

In the bath Wiliam found himself thinking of William bloody Fulbright, who had, it now occurred to him, loomed rather large over his childhood. He could not remember a time when he had not known about Will Fulbright.

'He was only twenty-two,' he remembered his mother sighing, while he had thought Only twenty-two, that's ancient, what's she on about? So I must've been, what, seven, eight? And catching up with him every birthday; he got younger every year. I grew up with him, thought William, sitting up straight in the water, he was like a sort of elder brother, a first son that had died, and me the next one, nice enough but never a replacement, oh no.

William lay down again and closed his eyes. He heard his mother run the hot tap in the kitchen. He let the house know that he was still on guard.

Go on then?

But still nothing happened.

Funny I've only just thought of it. But maybe everything I've done, all those exams, and Oxford, and Queen's Scouting and swimming bleeding certificates, perhaps I'd never have done it all without him. I'd thought it was her I was trying to impress, not her first old man. Or perhaps it was both of them: her past. I wanted to stop her preferring it to me. Was that it?

William snorted a little water in through his nose, and blew it out again, trumpeting.

And when I got to be twenty-three, I remember thinking it: Well, he never got this far, poor old William bloody Fulbright. And I could almost forgive him for being there all the time, and being better than everyone else just because he was dead.

Downstairs Binnie had heard the trumpeting and paused, her gloved hands in the water. It was the sound Eric made every morning, on finishing shaving. She would tell Eric about it some day, she thought; he would be so pleased. Though it would be best, she decided, not to tell him anything else about today. Certainly it would be simpler. Unless William's strange illness got any worse. Somehow she found herself unable to worry about this illness or even take it seriously. Working too hard and his girl's thrown him over; no wonder he got so excitable. It didn't sound like real madness, she thought. That had been pain taking over, not interesting hallucinations.

She went on scrubbing at something cement-like engraved on a sideplate. How important had it really been, her own actual madness? It had not lasted long, and almost no one knew of it; for years she had hardly thought of it. But had it, perhaps, made things different, more difficult?

I was always so frightened I'd hurt him. I'd go to touch him, brush his hair, and be tentative, he'd wrench himself away all irritable, perhaps because of that frightened touch? I've never met anyone else who's done the things I did.

'Look, I've got all this coal, all this coal, won't you take some?'

Binnie began to tremble.

Suppose I haven't been taken up with Will Fulbright at all. Suppose all that stuff about the first Will being the real one was irrelevant, that it was being mad that I was all taken up with. Because I tried to give him away, and I've never forgiven myself for it.

For a moment Binnie stood quite still, trying this possibility, savouring it.

But then, would she have gone so mad in the first place if Will had not died?

She went on scrubbing at the sideplate. All these truths, she thought. Ever since the letter, a whole queue of them had confronted her; they couldn't all be real, could they? How can I know, how can anyone know? All that stuff about suitcases, I thought I was being so clever, but it's just been misleading. They're not luggage or dogs stray or otherwise or packs of infinite cards, or all the other notions I've tried to turn them into. Figures of speech, thought Binnie, you have to be really careful with them. They make you think you've hit on something when you haven't. And she remembered a little doll her sister had once owned, a cloth doll that seemed to sit with its skirts prettily spread, its neat cloth toes just peeping from under the hem, and when you picked it up you realised it had no legs at all, just the toes sewn onto the skirt's single broad triangle. That's a figure of speech for you, thought Binnie, frowning with effort over the cooling greasy water in the sink. It's all pretty skirt, no guide at all to what's underneath, which might be legs or might be nothing at all.

But how else can you describe things? You can only keep

on trying, make the image stand as clearly for the real thing as you can, as if truth lies where the two are most alike.

So here's another go. I've got memories: like pictures drawn on sand. I thought I could pick them up for a closer look. I wanted to because of the Home, and because of the letter. But all I've found is confusion. Is that what you found, Dora, Mrs Bell?

For a moment Binnie hesitated, considering. Then she noticed the state of the water, exclaimed over it, dismissed what she had been thinking about, forgot it, and turned the hot tap on.

'Did you make some tea?'

'Yes. How are you feeling? Better?'

William nodded. It was true. Perhaps his mother's bizarre grief, he thought, had taken some of the force out of his own.

'Did you see any of your pictures?'

He winced, but answered mildly enough: 'No. They seem to have gone. For the moment,' he added, in case anything was listening.

Binnie poured out. The kitchen, William thought, looked almost absurdly clean and tidy, considering how short a time his mother had been at work in it.

'Your fridge needs defrosting. I had to throw nearly everything in it away.' She spoke indulgently, and he saw that she had been amused by the mess, found it fitting for a bachelor, and endearing, and all that sort of 1950s thing; as if he was something out of a TV sitcom, he thought irritably. He was conscious, however, of a strange desire not to offend or undermine her in any way, and managed to keep quiet.

'Do you often not go into work? Or was it because of, you know, seeing your pictures?'

'It wasn't pictures,' said William, annoyed by this (typical of her, he thought) piece of uncomprehending trivializing over-simplification, 'Anyway,' he went on more gently, 'no, I just didn't feel like it today, because of – my girlfriend. I found out last night you see, I called a friend of hers. Then I thought I'd go and see her this morning but she was out,' he went on uncomfortably. In fact he had not been told Laura's new address; had merely guessed at the area, and gone to hang about in it in the hope of accosting her on the street. Already it seemed a long time ago.

'What, you found out she was engaged last night?'

'Er, yeah.' Absurd term: engaged indeed. Shacked up, all right? But again, to spare her, he did not say this aloud. Nor did he explain the full extent of Laura's betrayal, in case it put his mother onto some track or other. For himself, thinking about it was too painful for him to have spent much time yet on whether Laura being pregnant again made things in general better or worse.

'Have one of these.'

'Er – I think they're Lewis's, Mum.'

'He won't mind, will he?' sniffed Binnie. 'You can always get him some more, can't you?'

Not from Vienna, no, thought William, resignedly helping himself.

'Though of course that's the sort of thing you mostly never get round to,' said Binnie happily, 'you know, like returning books that you've borrowed, or visiting places on the way back. You're going somewhere and you pass something, you tell yourself you'll call in on the way back. But you never do.'

William smiled with her. But at the same time he was

thinking: She was testing me. Laura. Perhaps she wasn't even sure she was doing it. But she took risks. She was testing me. Some test, that had ended for her in an operating theatre, with her legs strapped apart and metal things being poked inside her. Some price, for finding out how completely I would fail her. Has it been worth it, Laura? I wish you'd let me see you, but perhaps that's the sort of thing you wouldn't want me to ask. Has it been worth it?

Still, it doesn't seem to have done her too much harm. No prizes for guessing what she'd really wanted all along.

'Was it something to do with her, d'you think, you seeing those – pictures?'

William shrugged, admitting the possibility. Though within he was almost certain.

I obviously felt more guilty about it than I quite knew. Interesting what your mind can do for you. A classical punishment. Didn't I say those things to Laura, that someone once said to Jocasta? I made her cry, I made her listen. She did what I told her to, but even so it all came true. I made it come true. Jocasta is marrying someone else, and my child can still destroy me.

Oedipus' father. What was his name, anyway? Why couldn't I say Great, let's chance it! I loved her. Why couldn't I?

Because of Mum and Dad? He looked across at Binnie.

Who'd want to recreate that?

'You and Dad,' he said. 'What's it all about? Why d'you stick together? You don't like one another very much, do you?' He held his breath.

She was silent for a moment, though she did not seem surprised.

'He's got no joy in him,' she said at last. As an explanation of Eric she felt this had a lot going for it. You could be sorry for him and yet not sorry; he wasn't missing anything after all. And who could blame you, for quarrelling with a man who had no pleasures? She wished she had come up with this angle on him before. Still, it was a comfort to have caught on now.

'He's been worried about you,' said William, forgetting that he had not told his mother about his father's shamefully truncated telephone call.

But Binnie did not listen. 'We're all right,' she continued, as if he had not spoken, 'we get along. You get to be our age, you don't need so much from other people, you just need a little and we can do that much. You're young, you still need a lot.'

'I need too much,' said William rather cheerfully. 'I don't think I'm cut out for marriage.'

'Well don't leave it too long,' said Binnie, 'or people'll start thinking you're funny.'

'I am funny,' said William, smiling. 'I get it from my old mum,' he added, cheekily, tenderly. He had never spoken so to her before, but Binnie knew just how to reply.

'Get along with you,' she said, smiling back. Presently she remembered that Jean Shone next door was moving, and told him so, and he remembered playing 'A Guid New Year To Ane And A'' with the loud pedal down, and Mr Shone's black hairy T-shirt, and the hop-plants hiding behind the clematis.

It was the nicest afternoon either of them had spent for a very long time.

Twenty-Five

Julia had twigged. So she told herself.

Oh yes, I've twigged. What a joke! Though there was still plenty of scope for the opposite conviction: that William had really telephoned her first and Evie incidentally rather than the other way round. Two whole days, three nights and a morning had given Julia lots of time to change her mind in, and she had done so, exhaustively and faster and faster, so that by the time she knocked on William's office door at three-fifty-five on Wednesday she was alternately convincing and doubting herself every few seconds. It had come to be almost a comfort, as the ceaseless toing and froing had got so boring; it had been possible at last to include William himself in with the general boredom of endlessly thinking about him.

So Julia considered as she marched up the corridor wearing her own by now clean but ordinary jeans and jumper. But her heart jumped hammering into her throat as she knocked.

'Hallo.'

'Hi!' He had part of the headset round his shoulders. 'Hang on a minute, sorry – '

She remembered how she had heard him laughing in

here, and making mysterious animal noises all by himself while he played with his computer, and a sudden passion of longing for him made her feel slightly dizzy. Tell yourself what you like, she thought, that it's all nonsense I've made up, that it's only a fantasy of loneliness, that he's just a rather nice-looking ordinary chap: none of it makes any difference. A little congratulatory thrill ran all through her, for being so real.

'Don't want to stay in here, do we? Look. Tell you what. D'you want to see my garter snakes?'

Julia laughed. 'Where?'

'Here, of course. Well, in the woodshop actually. Upstairs.'

'All right then.'

'Enid and Charles, they are,' he said, leading her back down the corridor to the lift. 'Of course I didn't go into all the difficulties, not in the paper.' He bashed the lift call button. 'I mean, they're not exactly photogenic, they dislocate their jaws you see, so they can swallow whole sheep and things, and they kept doing it when I'd got them clamped into position.' They stepped out two floors up, and she followed him down the corridor again and up an unexpected flight of stairs at the end.

'And I couldn't keep their eyes open properly. Extra eyelid, see.' William took a key out of his pocket, knocked, paused, and turned the lock. 'There they are!' The woodshop smelt pleasantly of sawdust and schooldays glue. 'Hallo Enid! Hallo Charles! How are you? Look who's come to see you!'

The snakes, coiled into two neat piles, made no move.

'Are you sure they're all right?'

''Course they are. They're really pleased to see me. Aren't you, Enid? They're just playing it cool. They don't wear their hearts on their sleeves, garter snakes. Do you, lads?'

He smiled down at her. 'Pretty, aren't they?'

'You seem very happy?'

'Ah. Well. I've had this offer, you see. Between you and me. And you, Charley.'

'Oh?'

'Yup. Texas. Wrote to me: work in Houston.'

'What, your – '

'Computer. Funding. Students. Possibility of tenure.'

'Well, congratulations! Ah, when are you going?'

'Oh I'm not sure I'm going at all. I'm thinking about it. I couldn't get back, could I, afterwards. Anyway there's been hints from Japan as well.'

'Japan?'

'Yes. Interior decorating. Architectural design. You know, find out beforehand if you're really going to like your lounge done out in puce anaglypta, that sort of thing.'

'Gosh, when did – '

'Whereas Houston, be military. I reckon. Mock up Armageddon. Well, someone's got to do it, haven't they, Enid?' He turned back to Julia. 'I'll probably go for Texas actually. Bloody long way away though. I'll send you a postcard, shall I?'

'If you like.' Julia looked away.

'Here,' he said suddenly, changing tone. 'D'you happen to know what Oedipus' father was called?'

'What?' Startled, Julia considered. 'Um, I used to – no. I can't remember, sorry, why?'

'He's not really a very memorable bloke, is he?'

'Well, he does get killed rather early on. Doesn't he?'

'Yeah. I suppose he does. I'd forgotten that.'

A word came to Julia's rescue: *manic*. She felt a little

better now that she had defined his behaviour. She looked back at the snakes. 'What do they eat?'

'Oh, you know. Whole goats, live chickens. Chappie, mostly.'

'Well,' said Julia helplessly, 'they're very nice.'

'I knew you'd like them.' He beamed at her. It was true, he thought: he was happy. Whatever it was that had been happening to him, hallucinations, nightmares, seemed to have stopped; because he had told someone, confessed this particular strange weakness, faced its possible causes? Or because it was his mother he had told? It was as if he had given her a special present, he felt now, enjoying the generous glow of it. Though he was aware, too, that Binnie's standing had altered with him; tragedy gives you a sort of stature, he thought. Anyway he was safe again. He had even toyed, earlier, with the notion that his mother had somehow saved him, but this he had rejected, as going too far.

And he and Lewis had had supper together the night before, and Lewis had told him about the series of boardroom scandals and takeover bids that had prompted him to spend so many uncomfortable nights camped out on his office floor; and he had told Lewis about Laura, and understood that it would soon, or soon enough, be all right again, that he would be able to say her name without pain one day, that it was foolish to imagine there was only one Right One, when clearly there were dozens, and lots of Perfectly Useful Ones in the meantime while you were looking, if you were looking at all.

Which I'm not, thought William, noticing how prettily Julia's hair fell, swinging like a glossy bell round her slender face.

And because he was so happy, what with Texas and

Japan and so on, he put his hand on Julia's shoulder, turned her round, and gave her a nice warm kiss to remember him by.

It was a real kiss, thought Julia, still stunned, at home several hours later, while she waited for Evie to get her make-up on: a kiss so promising, so fertile, that recalling it she could perfectly understand why children often thought that kissing could make you pregnant.

'Er, are you all right?' he had asked her afterwards, standing back and looking quite concerned.

'Honestly, Eve,' Julia had called from her bedroom as she had zipped up Evie's black-and-white dress, which suited her so well, 'I nearly fainted with desire, I nearly passed out!'

'Berk,' Evie had called back affectionately. She and Mr Dull were all washed up again, but she wasn't depressed about it yet, she was still too cross. She and Julia were off out tonight on the razzle, to take their minds off things.

'Why can't you understand,' she went on, coming into the living room working her black lace gloves on, 'that the best men are the ones you fancy the third time you meet them?'

'What, like old Dull-features?'

'Don't you call him that,' said Evie, grinning. 'Look. D'you think these are too much?'

'Of course not. I don't suppose he'll call me, do you?'

'Bad news for you if he does, really.'

'Oh I don't know. There'd have to be a few good bits before it all went wrong, wouldn't there?' She remembered the kiss, and wondered if she would ever sleep again.

'They wouldn't be worth it,' said Evie, slamming the front door behind them.

They would, thought Julia mutinously, remembering other earlier sleepless nights. She stepped onto the path, and as she did do, the telephone began to ring inside.

'Evie! Quick!'

'Leave it.' Evie squeezed her keyring back into her bag. 'For God's sake,' she went on calmly, 'whoever it is can try again, can't he? If it's *him* he'll try again. He'll want to more, if you're out, it's strategy.'

The phone was still ringing.

'I can't bear it,' cried Julia, in partly real, partly mock agonies.

It rang again.

'Oh, Evie!'

And stopped.

Julia sighed. 'It was probably for you anyway.'

They set off for the bus stop.

'Oh gosh that kiss,' said Julia, 'I'll never forget him now, never.'

'Well, what's wrong with that? You've got to remember something, haven't you?'

'But it's not fair. He's not going to remember me.'

'Oh, don't be such a pain,' said Evie, but still friendly. 'I bet that was him calling. Bet you what you like.'

'But Evie – '

'Look, is that a 29?'

Evie hurried on ahead, her padded shoulders swinging. Julia let her go. Just you try any more outflanking manoeuvres, she thought at Evie's retreating back. Anyone interesting from the Arts Council or otherwise, you just keep your distance, thought Julia, smiling to herself.

'Hey it *is* a 29 – come on!'

Laughing, Julia began to run.